THE NEW YOUTH CORRIDOR

YOUR ANTI-AGING GUIDE TO TIMELESS BEAUTY

A fresh look at a renowned plastic surgeon's revolutionary program for prevention, maintenance, and correction

GERALD IMBER, M.D.

KCM PUBLISHING
A DIVISION OF KCM DIGITAL MEDIA, LLC

CREDITS

The New Youth Corridor by Gerald Imber

ISBN 13: 978-1-939961-52-5
ISBN 10: 1-939961-52-1

Author photograph by Mario Sorrenti
Publisher: Michael Fabiano
KCM Publishing
www.kcmpublishing.com

KCM Publishing
a division of KCM Digital Media, LLC

CONTENTS

Preface

"What in the world is the Youth Corridor?"

I consider the Youth Corridor that central pathway of adult life when you look your healthy, attractive…and yes…youthful best. The simple purpose of this book is to teach you how to extend that period for decades. The heart and soul of *the Youth Corridor* is my philosophy of prevention • maintenance • correction™; a common sense guide to helping you help yourself based on the best science and forty years of clinical experience. The program has been tried, proven, and vastly improved over the years. No fads, no fakes, no fooling.

This strategy, and the book it spawned, are meant to help guide people through all stages of life. The youngest among us, usually those who seem to need no help at all, can actually be the greatest beneficiaries of the program. Young adults have the ability to change the pattern of aging. They must learn how to avoid accelerating aging and how to retard its progress. Their reward, for a little bit of attention, will be a lifetime of looking their best. For those in early and middle adult years, the strategy will provide the necessary tools to help maintain youthful good looks. And for those of middle age and beyond, the book will clearly lay out all the options, invasive and noninvasive, for correcting and reversing the signs of aging and resetting the clock.

New concepts catch on when need and knowledge begin to fuel one another. Then a good idea takes on a life of its own. At that point things seem so obvious that we wonder why it took so long to happen. The Youth Corridor is that sort of situation. In the last two decades, science has become more active in combating aging as baby boomers turned their interest to the quality of life, rather than simply the pursuit of success. This confluence of events totally changed the landscape. Millennials picked up the ball and ran with it. The internet became a lifeline, expert, and not-so-expert bloggers crowded the superhighway provided by the web. Torrents of information became available from every source; some of that information has proven extremely useful, some erroneous, and some downright counterproductive. Science is a funny thing. Skimming the surface, one can cherry-pick facts and statistics to prove almost every point. Without expert fact-checking, information can run amuck. To make use of the worthwhile data, we need to fully understand the problems we are dealing with, have a sound base of scientific knowledge, and apply that knowledge in an organized fashion. That is what I will attempt to do in this book: organize the bits of helpful information floating around us into a systematic program for controlling aging and maintaining one's youthful good looks throughout adult life.

In my busy career as a New York plastic surgeon, I have performed more than fifteen thousand operations, including nearly four thousand face-lifts, and it's fair to say that I know skin inside out. Through these years I have been consumed with the very basic problem of how to control facial aging. My interest has taken the form of studying the unfolding biochemical and genetic advances; devising effective, less-invasive surgical procedures; and conceiving of the whole process of controlling facial aging as a series of related steps to reach a goal. Applied properly, these are initially small steps of self-help, augmented by bits of professional intervention as the years go on.

I have long preached the gospel of small procedures performed early, rather than waiting for the situation to get out of hand, and then seeking a miraculous transformation. For decades, colleagues in the plastic surgery community dismissed this strategy. That is no longer the case. The philosophy has now gained something close to universal acceptance; I often recognize my own words coming back at me, and it feels good to hear others preach what some of us have known to be true for decades.

Prevention makes sense. Self-help, good skin care, and noninvasive-help make sense, and smaller procedures, performed earlier, make sense and can keep you looking great throughout your adult years. Will all this actually prevent aging? No. Truly being able to prevent aging remains out of reach but what we know now will surely slow down the effects of time and help you enjoy your life looking your best. If this makes sense to you, read on—there is a lot we can do together.

With each edition of *The Youth Corridor* I try to provide the most up-to-date information available. One of the wonders of e-books is the ability to respond rapidly to changes, and things have certainly been changing. Since William Morrow published the first edition of this book in 1997, it has become something of a bible for those interested in prevention, maintenance, and smaller, less invasive corrections. A lot has changed over the years, and so has the book. *The Youth Corridor* is a look at what science has made available today, what makes sense, what doesn't, and how you can do the most to help yourself.

In this 2017 edition, the strategies incorporated in the book are the very same as those provided to our patients at the Youth Corridor Clinic. The Clinic has institutionalized these concepts alongside my cosmetic surgery practice to provide patients with expert advice and care well short of the need for surgery. With the assistance of a superb professional staff, chemists, skin care scientists, and the newest equipment we have evolved an organization that strives to provide the best individualized antiaging and beauty care imaginable. In this book, and in the clinic, I have no patience for phony claims, miracle machines, or magic pills. Nor do we jump on the bandwagon following every fad perpetrated by know-nothing hustlers. We have made it a mission to produce the most effective skin care products, the most modern, and least invasive treatments, and provide every patient with a road map of their needs now and for the future. In short, we have brought the concept of the Youth Corridor to life, and have expanded it to meet the needs of the modern men and women.

Obviously, even the most diligent study of these pages is not quite the same thing as sitting together and discussing what is best for you, and your future. But reading this book will help you understand the science of skin care and the natural process of aging and how to influence it. Using it as a reference tool, you will be better able to make proper choices, and I am confident that it will be time well spent helping you help yourself.

At the end of the book we have added space for you to jot down notes, reminders, and questions as you read. This may be particularly helpful in chapters 12 and 13. Feel free to contact us with any questions you might have anytime at:

www.youthcorridorclinic.com.

THE NEW YOUTH CORRIDOR

ONE

Introduction to the Youth Corridor

❝ ❙ was always happy with myself and the way I looked. I never seriously thought about changing anything. Sure, I didn't look as young as I used to, but it wasn't terrible. Then, one morning, I looked in the mirror and saw my mother. That was it. I love my mother, but I don't want to look like her...at least not now. When did all this happen? What do I do now?❞

That sort of question, and the accompanying frustration, provided much of the impetus for this book. Too many people have wasted too many good years helplessly watching the changes add up instead of fighting back. It's frustrating, it's annoying, and we have philosophically written these changes off as the legacy of genetics and the effects of time. Two generations ago there was little to do but grind our teeth and wait for things to get worse. Happily, that is no longer true.

Twenty-five years ago, I became obsessed with the idea that there had to be a better strategy than watching the horse leave the barn before closing the barn door. But what to do? I was fully aware of the problem, and the solutions available were purely surgical and aimed at correcting accumulated damage. But for most people it was too much, too late. Who wants to sit idly by and watch their youth slip away? Worse still, who wants to sit around and wait for aging to become pronounced enough to need the kind of old-fashioned, windblown, too-tight face-lift that has given plastic surgery a bad name?

When I first began to question this conventional approach, I was particularly struck by the absence of treatment options for the early changes of aging in younger people. Our professional attitude had been that these early changes weren't worth dealing with. That simply made no sense. It seemed to me that if we were going to influence the eventual outcome, the earlier we became involved, the better. Attention had to be paid to attending to, and preventing, the earliest signs of aging—avoiding wrinkles, not just trying to cure them—and not merely surgically reversing the established signs of middle age, but preventing them. Couldn't we reorganize the way we apply our knowledge to the problems of aging? Couldn't we use what we know of anatomy, cellular physiology, surgery, medicine, genetics, and the chemistry of skin care to help maintain vigorous good looks, instead of sitting around and watching youthfulness slip away?

Those were pretty much my driving thoughts as I altered and reorganized my priorities within my very traditional practice of plastic surgery. How wonderful it would be if people could maintain their youthful appearance throughout adulthood, middle age, and beyond. As a society, most of us no longer worry about simple survival. We live longer and better lives, and quality of life counts. When one has reached a stage of confidence and achievement, why not welcome it looking as good as one feels? The fact is, we are able to maintain an attractive and naturally youthful countenance for decades longer than prior generations. It is simply a matter of caring enough to make the effort. The information necessary to do so is available. Organizing that information in a helpful program requires understanding of the changes brought on by the years, and a willingness to apply the program at every stage of adulthood. You truly can look great throughout your adult life, and helping you do so is our goal.

The book you are about to read may actually change your life… well, at least it will help you look better. It is a compendium of the latest scientific advances in the control of facial aging, organized in an understandable manner, and presented in a fashion applicable to any age. The Youth Corridor method will help a twenty-five-year-old retain her youthful good looks by changing the pattern of aging well into the future, it will stabilize the thirty-five-year-old, offer maintenance and effective options for reversing signs of aging in the forty-five-year-old, and tell the fifty-five, sixty-five, and seventy-five-year-old how to reset the clock. Whatever your age, this information can help you look your best.

Obviously, the optimum time for prevention is before changes have begun. Those with enough insight to begin early are the lucky few; the rest of us must slow the process, undo the visible changes, and pay more attention to ourselves. There is so much to be learned. Simply eliminating negative influences is an important step in the right direction. If you come away from this book with new insight and an enlightened attitude, you will be on the road to helping yourself. Adopt the program at any stage of life, and you will truly do some good. The deeper you immerse yourself in the routine, the maintenance process, and yes, even the applicable procedures, the better you will look. It's as simple as that.

TWO

The Youth Corridor

Though the worlds of self-help, preventive skin care, and cosmetic surgery might seem clearly compartmentalized, increased overlap between the disciplines has blurred those lines. The anti-aging universe includes skin-care products; noninvasive skin-care treatments performed by estheticians and nurses in spa settings or doctor's offices; injectable fillers and Botox administered by doctors and nurses in all sorts of settings; treatments by dermatologists and plastic surgeons specializing in skin care; and cosmetic surgery that encompasses all of the above.

Every specialist, every effective product and technique, has a role to play so long as the information provided is honest, the products are effective, and the practitioners well-trained and knowledgeable. Unfortunately, some product claims skirt the truth, and some doctors are not qualified to perform the procedures they are promoting. But for the most part, professionals are well trained, don't overstep their level of expertise, and have your best interest at heart. Still, this is an area where promises, uninformed statements, and false claims are not infrequent. In this book I will try to guide you through this obstacle course and help you emerge at the other end looking your very best.

The Youth Corridor strategy has evolved gradually and has helped thousands of patients over nearly two decades. This book will explain it all to you. But be warned: Don't expect a generalized do-it-yourself book or a New Age paean to positive thinking, though the influence of both can be seen. There is no modern-day Ponce de León, no fountain of youth, and no doctor in a crisp white coat offering a magic potion with a benevolent smile. Forget it. That's just a dream.

All you are about to learn is the farthest thing from wishful thinking. It's real, and it works, which is largely because of the organization and expertise at the heart of the program. There is no one size fits all approach to antiaging and beauty. One must be expert in all aspects of the subject and present it in an honest approachable manner. To that end, much of what can be done consists of minor lifestyle changes, and new prevention and maintenance routines. The basis for what we will explore together is scientific. I may take some liberties of simplification in order to avoid confusion, but I intend to tell it like it is, and it's all about aging and how to control it.

Even as you read this, you should start with a positive attitude; scowling and sadness take their toll. There is a great deal you can do for yourself, much you can do with a bit of professional help—and yes, some that is possible only with professional help. You can accept or reject the elements of the Youth Corridor program as you wish. Even the simplest bits of reeducation will have positive results; but like a computer, what you get out of it depends on what you put in. This is reality, and if you want to keep looking the way you envision yourself—or perhaps even better—pay attention.

Age and beauty are often carelessly confused. Let us clear that up right away. Appearing youthful and beautiful should coexist, but you can have one without the other. We are interested in both. One person's vision of beauty is often shockingly different from another's, particularly across cultural boundaries. Beauty takes many forms. Among the Nuba tribes of central Sudan, intricate patterns of decorative body scarring are considered an important element of beauty for young women. Distortion of the lower lip with the insertion of increasingly large hockey puck–like objects is a crucial element among a largely primitive tribe in the Brazilian rain forest. But is that very different from the multiple tattoos adorning men and women today? Are the nose rings favored by Nubians significantly different from Western nose rings, eyebrow rings, navel rings or, for that matter, earrings? Beauty is a subjective and culture-dependent issue, which, for a while at least, is denied universality by the happy fact that the Earth is not yet a homogeneous planet. Differences still abound. Parents in America often seek plastic surgery for their young children with protruding tea-cup ears. Their reasons are understandable. Children are merciless in their taunting of deviations from the norm, and parents respond sensitively to their children's discomfort. But, in certain counties of Ireland, the majority of the native population boasts protruding ears, which are considered as handsome and normal as can be. Beauty is variable. Aging is an entirely different matter.

Though many Eastern cultures genuinely revere the elderly, they are, as a group, held apart from the bulk of active society. In Western culture, our productive years far outstrip our welcome in the workplace. Being old, or even looking old, signals exclusion from the active, productive segment of society, even when one has a great deal to offer. It is far worse when middle-aged individuals appear older and less vital than they are. We all recognize this and have seen the process in action. So it is no surprise that we all want to look young longer and fully enjoy what life has to offer.

Even the vainest among us grudgingly concede that there may well be a time to acknowledge age and let nature take its course. But the battle cry is, "Not yet! Not while I'm still young! Not while there is so much to do." This book is about maintaining your youth, and with it, your youthful appearance. With the proper program, you might well continue to look twenty-five or thirty when you are more than a decade beyond that point in life. It's ridiculous for a fifty-year-old not to look youthful and beautiful. The point is don't watch youth slip away as you pull at your skin and wish things were different. Make them different.

Americans are no longer old at forty, sixty or even seventy, and the concept of retiring from a profession or responsible job at sixty-five is a senseless waste of an experienced natural resource. At any age, feeling good is directly related to looking good, and the impression we make is how we are perceived. The two go hand in hand. Good looks and vitality count at any age, but particularly beyond the actual blush of youth. Those who look old and act old are treated differently from those who wear the years well. The average life expectancy for American males across all socio-economic and educational groups is 76.2 years; for females, 81.2 years. Having the time and interest to read this book assumes more concern with health and lifestyle, and a life expectancy that will far exceed those numbers. In fact, life expectancy for affluent Americans has reached 88.9 years for men, and 92.9 for women. More than fifty percent of individuals who reach the age of sixty-five can expect to live to eighty-five, and beyond. The economically and socially advantaged among us can expect to live far longer. We have learned some of the lessons of medicine, and most of us live generally healthier lives.

The first half of the twentieth century saw the dawn of modern medicine, with the ability to control and alleviate human suffering and disease. With the advent of antibiotics at mid-century, medicine had progressed from a science of observation and diagnosis to one of active intervention and cure. From that point in time to this, the advances have been too fast and furious to list. Happily, as the fortunate beneficiaries, we have assimilated the new order of things and now take it for granted as our birthright. That's the good news. We can anticipate and expect to enjoy unprecedented longevity. As this new reality becomes routine, our focus naturally shifts from survival to quality of life.

Diet, exercise, and fashion and, indeed, even cosmetic surgery have become accepted elements of modern life. We want to look good for as long as possible. It seems patently ridiculous for a thirty-five-year-old woman to watch her youthful good looks slip away, or for people in their forties, fifties, or sixties to tolerate unnecessarily sagging, wrinkled, aged faces. To look old, beaten, and devitalized, when one is anything but, makes no sense at all.

The visible signs of aging are manifestations of genetically determined changes in the skin and underlying structures, interacting with environmental elements, and lifestyle choices, which accelerate the process. The biochemical nature of aging is similar for all of us, even if the outward signs differ. Some of us suffer fine lines and wrinkles as early as our thirties. Others see only a minor loosening of the jawline at fifty-five. As you will come to understand, these are all manifestations of the same process. The objective is to keep these signs at bay and not allow them a foothold. With genes and environment working against us, we need an ample bag of tricks to stop these changes in their tracks, before the sum total becomes a picture of a vital young person trapped in old, ill-fitting skin. And that is what this book is all about.

The following chapters will explain how skin ages. Then we will identify specific trouble areas, show you how to spot your own potential problems and teach you how to prevent, control, and even stop them. You will learn an effective skin-care routine and a maintenance schedule that can keep you happily within the Youth Corridor, even as your contemporaries grow old around you. If you are lucky enough to begin fighting the battle while you are still young, the results will be that much more dramatic and last that much longer.

THREE

Fast Forward

To fully understand the Youth Corridor, you must first have a general understanding of how we age. The subject is not nearly as terrifying as it sounds, and I will try to keep the scientific mumbo jumbo to a minimum. After reading these chapters, you will be able to accurately predict how people will age and pinpoint what action should be taken in various cases. Truly, you will look at strangers in the street, recognize their problems and know what they must do to stay in the Youth Corridor.

The discussion in this chapter is confined to the skin and its structures, which will keep the information from wandering too far afield. But it's good to be mindful of the enormous impact of systemic good health—and certainly systemic illness—on the aging process and, therefore, on one's appearance.

Example: The hormone insulin is manufactured in the pancreas. A deficiency of insulin is the cause of the metabolic disease diabetes; sugar intolerance is its hallmark. Numerous other aspects of the disease are well documented, including occlusion of small blood vessels, which impairs blood flow. This may affect various organs over the years, including the small blood vessels nourishing the skin. Reduced blood flow through the small vessels of the skin results in reduced nutrient supply and impaired removal of metabolic wastes, which, in turn, causes loss of elasticity, thinning and oxidation of the collagen layer, and wrinkling. Simply put, diabetes can cause excessive and early aging of the skin. Is this the most worrisome effect of the disease? Certainly not. But the prematurely aged skin of diabetics demonstrates how important the overall state of health is in determining how one's skin will fare over the years. This sort of knowledge is fertile ground, and dealing with metabolic disease, along with cell and chromosome biology, will definitely change the way we think about aging and how we deal with it in the future. But for now we must apply today's solutions to today's problems.

There is no precise point in time when the wear and tear of life begins to take a visible toll on the skin, but there is usually some evidence of change in most people as they approach their early thirties. Shaking your head in disbelief? Think again—and look again. Those little squint lines or smile lines, or whatever euphemism we choose to hang on them, suddenly surface at about that time. So do the little horizontal forehead lines, the first lines under the eyes, and the ever-so-slight folds of extra skin in the upper lid. "Not so bad," you say. And right you are. But these are the first signs. From here on, the process quickens. Soon the smile lines are deeper and more numerous. They no longer disappear after the smile ends, and they actually seem longer and less pleasant. The skin of the upper lid continues to stretch and begins to look puffy even when you are well-rested and living virtuously. It might even be more difficult to apply eye makeup smoothly. You're thirty-five, thirty-eight or maybe forty-five, but the process is moving along. It started earlier—much earlier—and if we had been more knowledgeable and proactive, there is much that could have done to keep the process under control.

First, you must accept that the natural deterioration of the skin begins in your twenties, when the outward signs are absent and you still look great. At this point, your efforts to deal with the process will bear fruit in a future you haven't yet considered. The reality is that most of the readers of this book are farther down the road. Young people, the major potential beneficiaries of this knowledge, think it will never happen to them. Still, the starting point is less important than the act of starting itself. At any point of intervention, you will ultimately be better off than if you hadn't begun at all. This program is for everyone. What is most important is that you want to continue feeling good about yourself, and unless you live in a vacuum, you will agree that looking good plays a major role in feeling good.

FOUR

How It Happens

Think of the skin as a form-fitting garment, like tights, that hug your body, move when you move and as you move. After exposure to the elements, multiple washings, and thousands of bends and folds, the tights begin to sag at the joints and generally loosen all over. That's how your tights age; it's even worse for your skin.

Human skin is only fifteen to twenty one-thousandths of an inch thick—thinner than most fabrics. And there is a lot of it, about twenty square feet, and it weighs eight to ten pounds. The skin is not just dressing. It is an important functioning organ, made up of two distinct layers called the dermis and the epidermis.

The dermis, the deeper of the two layers, is the connection between the skin and the internal body structures. It relates not only to the fat on which the skin rests or the muscle below, but through its network of blood vessels to the heart, lungs, liver, and the distant endocrine glands, which secrete hormones and regulate body functions. These same blood vessels within the dermis nourish the skin. The nerves that transmit sensations back to the brain are in the dermis and, in the deepest reaches of the dermis, are the sweat and oil glands, which discharge onto the skin. The substance within which all these important elements reside is largely collagen. Ah, that magic word. Magic indeed, for it is the state of this collagen that determines the elastic fit of skin and the presence or absence of wrinkles.

This youthful adult face will be our starting point and our goal.

Collagen is a protein—a string of amino acids or small chemical groups—bound to other amino acids in chains. These protein chains are fiber-like and well-organized with their neighbors in a regular, and fairly predictable pattern. When the pattern is disrupted, broken down, thinned, or interfered with, wrinkles result. This damage to collagen can occur by repeated actions such as squinting, smiling, or pursing the lips, not at all dissimilar to repeatedly folding and unfolding a piece of paper until it is permanently scored. That is one way a wrinkle forms.

Within the collagen substance is a similar and related fiber called elastin. These fibers are responsible for the resilience and elasticity of the skin, in much the same way that elastic fibers produce the rebound and good fit of a garment. If these fibers are denatured, or weakened, by chemical or mechanical means a loss of elasticity results. Exposure to the ultraviolet radiation of the sun sets up a chemical process called oxidation that undermines collagen and results in loss of its vital properties. The oxidation is caused by the chemical activity of what are known as free radicals—in the simplest terms, free oxygen molecules looking for substances to hook onto and change. When these free radicals are not neutralized by antioxidants the collagen breaks down. Just as tights become baggy and ill-fitting as they lose elasticity, so does skin. Denatured collagen causes wrinkled, loose skin, which in turn creates everything from saggy eyelids to jowls to "turkey neck." Clearly, it is to our advantage to maintain the integrity of the collagen and elastic fibers, as they hold everything together.

By age thirty-five, the first significant changes are visible.

The superficial layer of the skin is called the epidermis. It is exceedingly thin, but it's the only part we see, so it had better look good. Unfortunately, the sins of the body are visibly displayed. The deepest level of the epidermis is called the basal layer. It is the only living portion of the epidermis. The basal layer produces cells called keratinocytes that migrate upward toward the surface, gradually transforming into a protective coat of dead cells called the keratinized layer, or stratum corneum. In healthy, young skin, the keratinized layer is shed before it heaps up. In older skin, the shedding process is slowed and a range of skin irregularities—dryness, superficial wrinkles, and blemishes, to name just three—may result.

It is this component of the epidermis that acts as a barrier to the outside environment and is always on display. It shows wrinkles, blisters from sunburn, becomes scaly, blotchy and dry and, when not properly cared for, makes our skin look weather-beaten and old. This keratinized layer is what we moisturize to the tune of billions of dollars each year. But it is not money wasted, because the dead cells of the keratinized layer plump up when water is applied and sealed in with a layer of moisturizer. This effect lasts up to twelve hours, and actually makes the skin look smoother and healthier. It is a fleeting and superficial treatment that has its place. But using moisturizers and makeup without treating the skin is much like covering a stale cake with fresh frosting.

In younger skin, the keratinized layer is shed regularly. The cells don't accumulate, and the epidermis functions as it was intended to function, as a protective barrier and mirror to the underlying dermis. One of the strategies effective skin-care routines employ is to exfoliate, or shed the keratinized layer, to help keep it supple, youthful, and wrinkle- and blemish-free.

The epidermis and dermis together make up the skin. They are integrally related to one another and crucial to our existence. The skin, as a whole, acts as a barrier against loss of body water and dehydration, and as protection from the entry of bacteria and environmental toxins into the body. It helps regulate body temperature by releasing perspiration, which evaporates and cools the skin, and by dilation of the blood vessels to release heat through direct transfer from the skin to the external environment. Constricting the blood flow in the skin retains heat when that is called for. The skin is a functioning body organ, and it is critical to maintain its integrity. Even as the skin ages, it continues to perform these vital functions well.

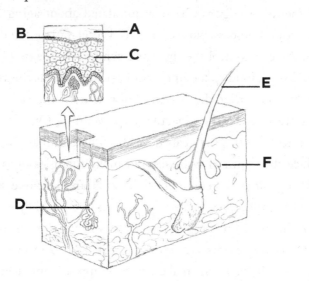

The schematic drawing represents a cross section through the human skin.

a. epidermis
b. basal layer
c. dermis
d. sweat gland
e. hair
f. sebaceous (oil) gland

The aging process of the skin is the sum of many factors. Chemical denaturing and oxidation of the collagen layer of the dermis is an ongoing phenomenon. It stretches, becomes less elastic and sags. Constant use also breaks down collagen in areas where it is folded, causing wrinkles. The blood supply to the skin, even without disease, becomes somewhat decreased and causes reduced nutrition and further breakdown of the collagen. Sun exposure accelerates collagen breakdown, and causes direct damage in the form of keratosis (scaly patches or lesions) and skin cancer. Various activities stretch the skin, including such benign things as leaning on one's palm while talking on the phone, or pulling at the skin with a towel. Soon enough, the elastic fibers break down. With time the skin thins, loosens, discolors, and wrinkles. And don't even think about smoking, and the damage that does. Not a pretty picture.

All the knowledge we have accumulated about aging cannot yet stop the natural process, but we can avoid accelerating it and even slow it down. We can control the signs and symptoms of aging before they start. And you can keep looking your best throughout the years, if you start early. The earlier the better. Unfortunately, the sad fact is that wrinkles are forever. The objective is prevention. Once wrinkles are written into the skin, they can never be fully eliminated. Though we can reduce the depth of wrinkles and make them less apparent, they still remain a singular reminder of the wear and tear one suffers over the years. Therefore, we must prevent them before they start. That is truly the thrust of this program, and you will learn much more about it later. New treatments are doing a great deal to reverse superficial wrinkles and, in fact, can make some disappear. But deep wrinkles, once they have set, are a more difficult problem. It is still fair to say that deep wrinkles are forever. That is why I suggest the use of Botox in younger people; to prevent early frown lines and smile lines from becoming indelible.

Facial folds and loosening, which are also manifestations of collagen and elastin breakdown, respond more favorably to surgery than do wrinkles, but they too are better controlled prior to becoming full-blown. Hence, I often suggest the early use of fillers or fat transfers.

I make it clear to my patients that it is impossible to eliminate all their wrinkles. It's easy to make skin fit properly, rejuvenate it, eliminate blemishes, lift sagging eyelids, reduce deep skin folds and generally make people look as if they are only just beginning to age. And, of course, I always hope to produce a marked improvement. But I never cease to be saddened thinking of those twenty years the patient spent helplessly watching the loosening and wrinkling become severe enough to bring him or her to surgery. Wasted years, waiting for the signs of facial aging to get worsen. And more frustrating, for doctor and patient alike, is the fact that at some point some of those things can never be reversed—or, at least, not fully reversed—and still look natural. It becomes all the more apparent that the time to pay attention is early…it is now. This theme cannot be emphasized often enough, and I will return to it repeatedly until it becomes as inevitable as aging itself. Our objective is maintaining your good looks. Follow the routine, make the little changes at the right times, and you might be lucky enough to keep right on looking great and never need a face-lift.

WHAT YOU SEE

Aging shows first around the eyes. That is the thinnest skin of the face and the most vulnerable to allergy, swelling, crying, and the wear and tear of expression. Some people begin to see this at twenty-five, but more usually it begins in one's mid-thirties. Often, these changes are accompanied by early, vertical frown lines between the eyebrows. Next comes the deepening of the nasolabial folds. That is the line from outside the nostrils to the corners of the mouth. Slight lines lead down from the corners of the mouth, sometimes accompanied by tiny pouches of fat. The occasional swelling beneath the eyes becomes bags, and the smile lines deepen. An occasional vertical line develops in the upper lip. Horizontal forehead lines may develop or deepen. Upper-eyelid skin becomes stretched and hooded, making you appear tired when you are not. Some wrinkles appear on cheeks, along with a few discolored spots. The lines leading down from the corners of the mouth seem to approach the jawline, giving the impression of jowls. The nasolabial lines deepen, and a bit of fullness and loosening develops in the lower face and under the jaw

We could follow the process further, but you get the idea. The sum of these changes, if you allow them to develop, would require a face- and eyelid-lift to undo, and despite all that, the deepest wrinkles would persist. Depending on one's genetic makeup, all this would typically take place by fifty-five to sixty years of age.

But why sit idly by and watch it coming, when a little self-help and maintenance can keep you in the Youth Corridor and looking great? True, you would have had to pay attention to lifestyle and skin care over the years, and yes, for the absolute optimal results you may actually require some form of intervention, even cosmetic surgery along the way. But you will have looked your best for those important years from thirty-five to sixty, or seventy. You won't be wrinkled or sagging, and you can continue to look the way you feel: young, healthy, and attractive.

FIVE

Prevention

Prevention is for everyone.

The objective here is to interfere with the pattern of aging. Young or old, you can always prevent things from getting worse. Of course young people will reap lifelong benefits from prevention…but the rest of us will get our money's worth as well. So many things we do in life to give us a moment's pleasure—or seemingly benign neglect—can do serious damage to our skin and, therefore, our appearance. We are obliged to step back and look at the effect of our lifestyle on the aging process. In addition, modern skin-care products have been proven effective in preventing, decelerating, and even reversing many of the visible signs of aging. To ignore these simple steps is to deny yourself years of looking good. If you don't really care, stop reading now. If you are like the rest of us and have an interest in helping yourself, it's time to get serious.

Understanding when to begin the routine is not very difficult. Start now! It's much like dressing for the day. The sensible person chooses clothing according to the weather, not the calendar. It's the same with a topic such as this. Don't wait for your thirty-fifth birthday and don't wait until changes are obvious. The worst that could happen in getting involved with the program too early is that you will have established good habits. If you choose to consult with your doctor about the program, you will be reassured and will have opened up a line of communication that will later prove invaluable. When I tell patients they are not proper candidates for a particular surgical procedure, I emphasize the fact that my business is doing surgery, not denying it. If I think a procedure is inappropriate, they should recognize the honesty of the response. Human nature being what it is, often this advice is ignored, and patients go from doctor to doctor until they hear what they wish to hear. If you want surgery, you will certainly find someone willing to perform it, but it is not always the answer. And when we are talking about prevention, there is no place for surgery. At the Youth Corridor Clinic, we see a significant number of young patients. Part or what we provide is education, along with an immediate plan, and a five-year plan outlining what sort of changes they can expect, and how to deal with them. I find that making things concrete helps make them real. I will make every effort to do that in the upcoming chapters of this book. Professional help aside, this book will help you help yourself.

You have nothing to lose and everything to gain by making small lifestyle alterations and beginning early maintenance. So let us get started.

The first and most important step is taking a close and clinical look at yourself. If you haven't already done that, then in all likelihood you are either too young to care or your appearance is simply not that important to you. There are probably people truly of the latter persuasion, but they are few and far between. Often this disclaimer of not caring is a cover for an unfortunate sense of futility, a place to hide. Most of us do care. Tastes and styles vary, and you may not be willing to commit yourself to this sort of endeavor, but I believe the majority of you have interest enough to read on. The objective of this section is identifying the changes of aging, not treating them, and some changes may be visible already, depending on where you enter the loop.

Now, back to that first look. If there are irregular areas of color or texture on your skin and you need the help of moisturizers or cosmetics to return its lost luster, then the changes of adulthood have begun—and it is the time to start. Fine lines about your eyes are early signs as well. At this point, you can still undo most of the changes and achieve great results with skin applications alone. If frown lines or smile lines are becoming part of your face, you're a bit past the pure self-help stage; nothing major is needed, but it is time to start. If there is a hint of the family double chin, it is time to deal with the problem while the easiest solutions and best results are possible. All of these are among the early visible signs of aging, and they respond well to the most basic care: in some cases, over-the-counter topical agents; in others, medical treatments; and in yet others, minor surgical procedures.

Whatever the case, if you want to forestall further changes, this is the time to take action.

Prevention is the first step. True regulation of the aging process is largely genetic. The intrinsic aging speed of our skin is determined by numerous hereditary factors, as well as individual response to aging accelerants in the environment—particularly the number-one culprit, sunlight. Others, such as smoking, stress, inflammation, and lack of exercise are significant players as well. All together, these factors are responsible for the individual pace of aging. At some point, for everyone, the machinery simply wears out, the skin loses its resilience, elasticity, and luster, and the signs of aging appear. That point becomes increasingly philosophical as science edges forward and aging is pushed farther along the curve. There is overwhelming evidence that aging of living organs is regulated to some degree by a tail, or cap, that exists at the end of each chromosome, called the telomere. Chromosomes are paired strings of amino acids configured in a double helix, the DNA described by Watson and Crick in 1953. At the ends of each chromosome are tails made of amino acids that have been described as the plastic tips on shoelaces that keep them from unraveling. These tails are called telomeres. Telomeres are longest in youth, and are intricately involved with cellular life. Living cells mature and wear out, and must be replaced by new cells. This cell turnover, or cell division, renews the vitality of the living organ; however, with each cell division, the telomere shortens. When it is shortened below critical length, the cell wears out, ages, and dies. Maintaining telomere length is the secret to eternal youth of the cell, and scientists working with gene-altering techniques have managed to introduce the enzyme that protects telomere length into experimental situations. The worry has been that the only cells known to be able to divide endlessly without aging are cancer cells. Is that what we are trying to mimic? Most recently, scientists have been able to replicate a short-acting substance that increases telomere length over a period of days and then dissipates, reducing the fear of reproducing the possibility of cancer like growth while returning youth to a waning cell.

This work with telomeres is particularly applicable to organs with fast cell turnover, like skin, and offers a bright star to guide us in manipulating the process of aging.

Other, very interesting, longevity studies have found that calorie restriction encourages longevity on the cellular and organism level. This has been proven repeatedly in mice and, in July 2009, graphically demonstrated, over the long term, in monkeys. A 20-30% calorie reduction is a worthwhile sacrifice if disease free longevity is assured. It isn't. We are not microorganisms, or mice, and not quite monkeys. So what may well make sense is not yet proven. A 2012 study from the National Institute of Aging disputes these longevity claims, while another primate study published in 2015 confirms the value of calorie restriction, further confusing the matter.

Few are inclined to live so ascetic a life as necessary to affect the benefit of severe calorie restriction, but a chemical in the skin of grapes and in red wine, called resveratrol, seems able to mimic the cellular benefits of severe calorie restriction, greatly increasing life span and physical well-being. The trouble is no one knows how much resveratrol is necessary to do the job. Laboratory mice demonstrated dramatic objective rejuvenation after being fed enormous amounts of the stuff. No one knows how much humans would require. Nonetheless, resveratrol supplements are flooding the market, and a lot of smart people are taking it despite the probability that the dose is quite insignificant. "Better than nothing," they say. Lots of money is being spent on research, but so far there is no reason to get excited.

The genetic, chemical, and mechanical causes for skin aging, and the research into controlling it, are interesting on the biological and chemical level, but for our purposes we have to deal with what we see, and what we can do about it, now. The visible changes of what we think of as aging, will be dealt with in depth in the following pages. We know a few basic facts about aging skin, which should direct our behavior and prevent accelerating the process. These simple lifestyle measures will not stop the clock, but they will definitely make an enormous difference.

THE TEN BIG TOPICS FOR PREVENTION

1. Don't smoke.

By now everyone knows this, but it demands reinforcement. Smoking constricts small blood vessels and reduces blood flow to the skin. The result is a decrease in nutrients and oxygen to the skin, and oxidation and denaturing of collagen. That causes loss of elasticity, sagging and wrinkles. It's as simple as that. The evidence is so clear that most plastic surgeons won't perform face-lifts on smokers—the blood supply to the skin is so compromised that portions of the skin are actually at risk of dying. This problem doesn't appear in nonsmokers. That's how severe the damage can be. Add to that the vertical lines that develop in the lips from puffing away, and you can see some measure of the damage you are doing to yourself; all this without mentioning the risk of lung cancer and cardiovascular diseases so closely associated with cigarette smoking. On the most basic level, smoking is very closely associated with telomere shortening and cell death. Science is telling us something.

2. Don't gain and lose weight repeatedly.

Maintaining a relatively constant weight makes great sense for a host of reasons. For our purposes, it is important to avoid the stretching of the skin caused by weight gain, and the laxity that follows weight loss. At some point, we can no longer get away with this. The skin loses just a touch of elasticity and doesn't snap back as quickly. That is the first warning signal. People in their thirties and forties are well advised to lose weight very slowly, not simply for physiological reasons but also in order to give the more slowly reacting skin a chance to shrink and fit the underlying structures. Slightly later in life, even this won't help. At this point, the skin will not respond to weight loss by shrinking, and will look loose, empty and haggard. Not a very nice reward for having the fortitude to lose weight. The older you are, or the more weight you need to lose, the more likely this problem will arise. Weight loss of more than a few pounds should be at the rate of half a pound per week. It is quite acceptable to lose two or three pounds the first week, as that is primarily water. After that, moderation is crucial. The lesson, of course, is to avoid significant weight gain, lose slowly and, above all, find your optimal weight and maintain it.

3. Don't get too thin.

Yes, you can be too thin. Hollow cheeks and thin skin may work for nineteen-year-old fashion models, but it makes an adult look frail, weak, and old. And there is nothing at all attractive about the look of anorexia. In fact, normal subcutaneous fat does much to plump out wrinkles and help the skin look and feel healthy. I am not proposing obesity, but you can surely be too thin. Consideration of the possible benefit of calorie restriction aside, being excessively thin is simply unattractive in an overall sense.

4. Don't run... *Hear me out!*

I know everyone's doing it. I know it feels great and has great mental and physical benefits, but that doesn't make it right. At very least, don't be a long-term, long-distance jogger. Take a look at the serious runners you know who are in their mid-forties, or fifties. Serious runners of normal weight have haggard, sunken faces, due primarily to a loss of subcutaneous fat. It takes a while to manifest itself, but that is the price extracted for the benefits running offers. All this becomes particularly obvious as the natural loss of facial volume occurs in the middle years. Thin becomes gaunt and aged.

Just as with any weight loss, the total reduction of body fat that results from running affects the face first. First the face, then the breasts, then the buttocks and abdomen. Running is more specific still in the loss of facial padding. The constant rising and pounding down, rising and pounding down, lifts and pulls the facial skin away from the underlying muscles and bones. You surely have seen this in slow-motion films of runners. The skin rises and falls, and as the foot impacts, it continues to fall for another fraction of a second, then bounces up again. The elastic fibers in the skin absorb the repeated trauma until they eventually cease to fully bounce back and ultimately stretch a bit, causing laxity of the skin. We all lose facial volume with age, but the combination of excessive loss of fat padding on the face, and accelerated loss of elasticity, have a decidedly negative impact on one's appearance. Jogging bras are universally worn for comfort and support against the tearing effect of the constant trauma of bouncing. Facial skin suffers the same fate, and yet it goes unprotected. Add to the brew arthritic knees, ankles, and backs, and one would doubt running is the aerobic exercise of choice.

The only positive that must be noted beyond aerobic health and the emotional high, are recent studies that linked increased bone density to the high impact activities such as running and jumping. Still, there is a price to pay.

It is not my intention to indict limited-frequency, limited-distance running, but be on guard. The beneficial effects of running are undeniable, but for most people low impact activities like biking, swimming, walking on the inclined treadmill, elliptical trainer, or stair-climber offer equal benefits with fewer pitfalls.

5. Exercise, Exercise, Exercise.

Exercise is crucial for life and longevity, but it also keeps skin biologically youthful and good looking. It has long been known that exercise increases circulation, builds muscle, and is a building block for a healthy and attractive body. Recent studies have shown that aerobic exercise as basic as working out on the stationary bike three times a week makes a world of difference. At the start of this interesting study, individuals sixty-five and older had facial skin biopsies before beginning training. As could be predicted, the outer layer of their skin, the stratum corneum of dead cells, was thicker than that of younger people, and the dermis, the layer containing collagen, was thinner. After three months of moderate training, as described, new biopsies showed the outer layer of skin thinner and healthier, and most importantly, the dermis thicker and healthier, and overall virtually indistinguishable from the skin of twenty to thirty year olds. If that isn't enough to get you on the bike, what is?

6. Facial exercises are a wrinkle workout!

Don't do them. They cause wrinkles. The facial muscles, or muscles of facial expression, are that group of muscles that originate on the facial bones and end, or insert, in the skin. They are thin, flat muscles that are just beneath the skin and serve to animate the face, or give it expression; hence the name. To understand how they work, try this: Tighten the orbicularis oculi muscle. That's the muscle that encircles the eyes and makes up much of the bulk of the eyelids. Tightening the muscle makes you squint.

Now do it again in front of the mirror. The squinting pulls the skin into wrinkles alongside your eyes. Now look in the mirror and smile and frown. The muscles of facial expression are attached to the skin, and repeated tightening, or exercising, of those muscles folds the skin over and over until wrinkles form.

Don't stop smiling. It's very human and very attractive, and it's a lot different than doing a wrinkle workout. The idea behind facial muscle exercises is surely well intentioned, but it's ignorant of anatomy. One day, when I was teaching facial anatomy to a class of first-year medical students at Weill-Cornell Medical College, I whizzed through the anatomy of the muscles of facial expression, and then prepared for questions. One of my students asked how facial exercises, which had become quite popular, actually worked. It made me think, and I told them what I tell you. Facial muscle exercises are nonsense. The attachment of facial muscles to the skin graphically reflects our expressions. That is why they are called muscles of facial expression. Exercising them in no way enhances the tone or strength of the skin and, when done repeatedly, the movement indelibly etches wrinkles into the skin. Deeper facial muscles have little to do with facial skin tone, and exercising them is generally a waste of time. Facial muscle exercises are a wrinkle workout, don't do them.

Notice smile lines at the corners of the eyes and on the cheeks and between the eyebrows. This is how facial muscles work.

7. Avoid the sun.

Nothing new or revolutionary here. Besides causing skin cancer, exposure to the sun is the primary accelerator of the breakdown of collagen and elastic fiber, causing loosening and wrinkling of the skin. If all this wasn't enough, the sun also causes pigment changes, sunspots, and various other unsightly eruptions. The intangible allure of a bit of color should be tempered with common sense, as there is absolutely no question that ultraviolet rays accelerate skin aging. Worse still, the effect is cumulative. Those days at the beach without sunblock will surely be paid for tomorrow, and the wise person would avoid adding today's insult to yesterday's injury. So the obvious decision is limited exposure. Cover up, stay inside, and slather on that sunscreen. The topic of sun protection will be dealt with in much greater depth in the section on sunscreens.

But the issue is much more complicated and important than the simple "just say no" implies. The problem is vitamin D. A cholesterol precursor of vitamin D is activated in response to exposure to sunlight on the skin, and then converted by the liver into the active form necessary for healthy bones. It doesn't happen in the dark. Vitamin D is essential to maintain the body's calcium balance. Calcium is necessary for many physiological functions within muscles, the immune system, and internal organs. Without adequate vitamin D, calcium is mobilized from the bones, resulting in reduced bone density. Decreased bone density leads to osteoporosis, brittle, thin bones, and fractures. Vitamin D deficiency in children leads to a condition known as rickets, in which bones do not calcify properly and become weak and bowed. Physicians and nutritionists complacently thought that decalcified bones were a thing of the past, but osteoporosis has become ubiquitous, particularly among postmenopausal women. This is the same osteoporosis we hear about endlessly on television, and apparently no one is immune. Calcium intake itself has been estimated to be inadequate for more than fifty-five percent of the population.

The issue may be that sunscreen protects the skin but blocks out the UVB spectrum of the sun necessary to produce vitamin D. So the question is: Protect against skin aging and skin cancer, or produce adequate vitamin D for your bones? Obviously a compromise is necessary. Most experts believe that ten minutes of midday sun on the face, arms, and legs three times a week during spring and summer is adequate for vitamin D production and bone health, as well as storage of enough vitamin D for the winter. The farther north one goes, the less potent the sun. Also, the darker one's skin, the less vitamin D produced by exposure, with the skin pigment acting as a sunscreen. But even individuals with outdoor lives and excessive sun exposure do not appear immune to inadequate vitamin D levels, and many experts recommend vitamin D supplements.

The standard recommended dose of vitamin D supplement had been 400 international units (IU). Many experts believe that is inadequate for most adults, and recommend 800-1000 IU daily for older people, whose skin is significantly less efficient at vitamin D production. After menopause, the larger doses are recommended as well. Excessive vitamin D intake has significant toxicity. The Institute of Medicine established the upper level of safety at 2000 IU daily. The Linus Pauling Institute at Oregon State University put the upper limit of safety between 5000 IU and 10000 IU, and recommends a daily adult dose of 2000 IU. I recommend a more conservative approach and, for those who get virtually no sun, a daily supplement of 1000 IU.

The whole thing is very confusing, and no one knows what is actually optimal. For now, drink milk, get a few minutes of sun, and take an 800 IU supplement if you cannot.

8. Nutrition.

Change your diet! This absurd generalization is still far more universally applicable than it should be in our information-rich society. Since the majority of readers, women or men, are individuals concerned with their appearance, you would expect this group above all others to understand and follow healthy eating habits. Not true. The majority of Americans are either overweight or on weight-gaining/losing yo-yo diets. The metabolically thin individual can get away with careless and excessive eating habits. The chronically overweight are bearing a potentially lethal load. For different reasons the chronically diet-thin represent an equally precarious situation, which leaves a fairly small minority of well-nourished, consistently thin individuals free from eating disorders, hormone imbalance, and calorie-counting.

Anyone old enough to be interested in this book has been nurtured on overindulging in an unhealthy pattern devised for us by authority figures and condoned by the government. A full measure of the burden of guilt lies with the medical profession at large—not intentionally, of course, but by complicity and avoidance, compounded by lack of understanding and inadequate knowledge and attention to facts that one can hardly avoid. The leading cause of death among American males is heart disease. Women, especially postmenopausal women, are increasingly close behind. Among the root causes of the epidemic of heart disease is very likely diet. Though the importance of other risk factors such as heredity, smoking, and lack of exercise cannot be underestimated, the fat-rich American diet is terminally related to the problem and is a reversible component in many cases. Study after study shows a rise in heart disease with introduction of fat-rich Western diets. Asians, boasting a negligible incidence of heart disease, develop increasing evidence of coronary artery disease as they assume Western dietary habits. Primitive cultures existing on vegetarian, animal-fat-deprived diets are free of significant heart disease until they are introduced to the bounty of civilization.

Over the last decade we have become more aware of the role played by the various kinds of fat, particularly in coronary health. The villain of villains is trans fat. This little devil is an integral component of most prepared foods and cakes. It lasts long and makes things taste good, and prevents them from becoming rancid. It also raises LDL "bad" cholesterol and causes plaque in the coronary arteries. Some of us remember butter substitutes, and how we were told they were healthier that natural, fatty butter. Well, as it turns out, those "healthy" substitutes were using trans fats instead of naturally occurring fats, and were doing far more harm than good. The case against trans fats is strong, and food companies, after complaining that there was no other way to ensure shelf life, have largely abandoned trans fats and found safer alternatives.

Monounsaturated oils like olive oil, peanut oil, and avocado are healthy and central to the much touted, Mediterranean diet.

Polyunsaturated fats like fish oil, corn oil, and safflower oil contain omega3 and 6 fatty acids, and are thought to be truly heart smart, acting in a protective manner, and often helping reverse heart disease.

In fact, there have been numerous low-fat dietary programs that have helped reverse heart disease with diet and exercise. Examples are legion, and the topic represents a book of its own. The point here is to direct you to reasonable eating habits. A diet that can kill you is certainly unhealthy, but it is unhealthy in so many insidious ways that the damage almost seems unrelated to the cause. It's hard to register that the eating habits with which we grew up are wrong. We simply ingest too many calories for the work we do. We are continually over-fueling the machine. And too much of the fuel is derived from fat. Besides being a source of cholesterol and cholesterol building blocks, each gram of fat contains nine calories, while each gram of carbohydrate or protein contains only four. So in addition to basic health hazards, fat delivers more than twice the calories per unit of the other food sources. That alone is cause for change. We eat too much, and we eat too much of the wrong things.

A simple strategy to encourage fat burning is *intermittent fasting*. If one skips breakfast…and there is no scientific reason not to…the sixteen hour period from dinner to lunch is long enough for the glycogen supplied by the previous day's carbohydrates to become depleted, forcing the body to metabolize fat for energy. It makes sense on many levels. Weight control, control of hyperglycemia, and it might just make you feel better and more energetic. An interesting side bar to the intermittent fasting story is the recent finding that human growth hormone levels skyrocket during the intermittent fasting period. A burst of natural hormone that increases lean muscle mass and reduces circulating triglycerides.

The effect of all this is both obvious and implied. Good health may not always be reflected in one's appearance; ill health often is. But overweight and out of shape is not attractive. Assuming we all understand the health value of proper weight maintenance, cyclical weight gain and loss is a hazard to one's appearance. Elastic and collagen fibers become increasingly unforgiving with the years. A twenty-pound weight fluctuation first stretches skin, and then leaves loose skin in its wake. Small weight loss without rapid regain is well tolerated at any age. Larger weight loss must be spaced over months to allow the skin to compensate. Obviously, the greater the necessary loss, the less likely the skin will shrink to fit. The best tactic is to achieve one's optimal weight and stay there. That needn't be model slim or unrealistically small for who you are. Maintain a good and healthy level that your body can comfortably adhere to.

Over the years, I have often been called upon to give diet advice. The truth is I have learned as much as I have taught, and if one is to have any lasting success with dietary changes, several rules must apply:

a. The plan must be easy.

b. There must be a sizable early result to fire enthusiasm.

c. The goals must be clearly defined and within reach.

d. The transition from "a diet" to your diet must be gradual and natural or it will not become part of your new lifestyle.

The plans I suggest may be no more effective, and certainly less radical, than those you have already tried—which speaks to the real problem. You shouldn't have needed more than one "diet." Over the short haul, they all work. Even four grapefruits and a prune a day will do the job for a week or two. The real issue is stabilizing your weight. That means forever. A fluctuation of three or four pounds is often seasonal or psychological and perfectly acceptable. Such a small amount, two to three percent of body weight, is easily shed without consequence. Maintenance requires a whole new mind-set. In order to be effective, it should require no thought at all once the changes have been learned. The following points have repeatedly proven their value. They are simple, painless, and in no way interfere with the enjoyment of food or the social aspect of meals.

But let's begin by revisiting the heretic concept of skipping breakfast. It's a difficult habit to shake, since it has been drilled into our heads that breakfast is the most important meal of the day. It isn't. And the *intermittent fasting* not only sets up fat burning, but also lowers triglycerides and LDL, the artery blocking bad cholesterol. I began skipping breakfast decades ago as a surgical resident. I felt sharper and more alert if I hadn't eaten. Carrying this over to decades of plastic surgery practice, I rarely eat until the day's surgery is complete. Skipping breakfast makes me feel sharper (no pun) and more alert. I also tend to eat less at lunch after skipping breakfast. Part of this is intentional…will power…and part due to hunger being abated by the chemical effects of the short fast. Over the course of the day I eat a full complement of calories, and virtually all foods that appeal to me, and my weight hasn't varied significantly in thirty years.

a. Begin every meal by drinking a full glass of water. It will slake some of the immediate hunger. Water takes up space, it has no calories, and it's good for you.

b. Eat salads as the first course—not, as in the European tradition, after the main course. The purpose is obvious. Salad is filling and, bite for bite, far lower in calories than anything that will follow. Salad dressings are fine, and the health benefits of olive oil cannot be overstated. Use it.

c. Eat half of what is on your plate, then stop and think. You are no longer hungry, so why keep shoveling the calories in? Always leave food over. The portions we are served or serve ourselves are unnecessarily large.

d. No second portions. Period.

e. No desserts.

f. Between-meal snacks should be limited to low-calorie drinks, preferably water, and fresh fruit. An apple, in addition to tasting great, provides complex carbohydrates, which are digested slowly and, through feedback mechanisms, repress hunger far longer than prepared snacks made with refined sugar. Fresh fruit contains far fewer calories than snack food and is rich in vitamins, nutrients and naturally occurring antioxidants.

Obviously, one should be concerned with the quality of food consumed. Fruits and vegetables are critically important. Anyone reading this book already knows that. Fat and cholesterol in all forms should be controlled, and trans fats banished. Most of all, calories do count. Yes, exercise burns calories and even raises your basal metabolic rate a bit for a couple of hours afterward, but is not an excuse for overeating.

Don't overestimate how many calories you are burning. An hour of tennis singles burns off barely 250 calories. Fewer calories than a Snickers and a Coke. Running a ten-minute mile consumes only 145 calories. Weight is controlled by taking in (eating) only enough calories to support baseline body requirements plus physical work. This means far fewer calories than one would imagine. Happily, it can all be managed with ease, if one is devoted to the task. A forty-five-year-old woman, five-feet-five-inches tall, weighing 110 pounds, needs about 1,600 calories daily for weight maintenance. Find a food calorie chart on the Internet and learn the basics. It will confirm what you already know about most foods.

The body mass index (BMI) is a good indicator of total body fat and is calculated based on height, weight and age. Federal guidelines suggest a BMI of 24 or less as an appropriate and healthy goal. There are BMI calculating services on the Internet. Plug in your statistics and see the truth. The rest is common sense. Find the right level for you and stick to it. The few tricks offered above will help, but remember: This is a maintenance aid, not a quick weight-loss diet. It's about painlessly changing your life style.

9. Learn about antioxidants and free radicals.

Talk about skin and you have to talk about free radicals and antioxidants. Free radicals are everywhere. They are unavoidable, and are now understood to be crucial issues in the health and beauty of one's skin, so pay attention. Free radicals are atoms with an extra electron in their outer layer. In this case, oxygen, with an extra electronic charge that allows them to enter into destructive chemical bonds with organic substances such as proteins. The result is oxidation, or chemical burning, of the substance, which destroys it. Protein becomes denatured, genes may be broken, and dangerous residual substances may result from the chemical changes. Large scale, visible examples of oxidation in daily life include the rusting of an iron grill left in the atmosphere, the quick browning of peeled potatoes, or sliced peaches, or avocados left in the open air. It is of interest for our later conversation to consider that when a sliced avocado or peach or potato is treated with lemon juice (a source of the antioxidant vitamin C), it does not brown. But before we jump to the conclusion we are hoping for, immersing them in water inhibits the oxidation as well. Knowledge of all this has been around for a long time, though only recently has the process become a consuming interest of researchers and health faddists alike. At the same time that the destructive capabilities of free radicals were becoming known, many compounds that combat this destructive oxidation were identified. They are known as antioxidants, and include among their number many vitamins that were thought to be healthful even before the reasons were clarified. Paramount among these is vitamin C.

Various activities of daily life have been shown to increase the presence of oxygen free radicals associated with destructive oxidation. Exposure to sunlight is known to lead to oxidative destruction of the skin, including increased incidence of skin cancer and the collagen-destroying processes causing wrinkling. Strenuous aerobic activity has been associated with increased free radical formation. But, while athletes produce more free radicals, they may have also developed a more effective method of combating the damage with natural antioxidants. Some new science has muddied the waters by claiming a healthy role for free radicals in normal metabolism, particularly as related to strenuous exercise. The whole picture is less clear than had been thought, but the evidence of free radical production leading to oxidation and tissue damage is real; some of the findings are confusing, they always are in science, and we are only just scratching the surface of understanding a very important mechanism.

Vitamin C has been given credit for all sorts of miracles, proven and unproven. It is a potent antioxidant and a necessary component of tissue collagen production. Again, we are advised that normal diets, including citrus fruit, provide adequate vitamin C. Over the years scientists and clinicians have waffled over claims of the ability of vitamin C to prevent colds and lessen the length of time that symptoms persist. It is generally believed that these qualities are overstated or wrong. One study did show vitamin C to be effective in preventing cold symptoms in fifty percent of marathon runners tested, but this was only a tiny percentage of the general population. Since I'm so set against subjecting one's body to marathon running, I nearly opted to leave that bit of information out. The significance of this remains unclear. What is increasingly clear is that the final chapter has not been written.

Antioxidants, such as vitamin C, are key players in preventing the formation of cholesterol plaques in the arteries and are generally necessary for sustained good health. The importance of vitamin C is well-known for its role in the healing of wounds and maintenance of the integrity of tissues. It is critically important in collagen synthesis, and its absence causes the disease scurvy, which results in tissue breakdown and open wounds. In the past this was a common condition suffered by sailors during long sea voyages. The association of citrus fruit, rich in vitamin C, with prevention of the disease led to British ships carrying stores of limes for consumption on extended passages, hence earning British sailors the nickname "limey."

For most people excess vitamin C is quickly and harmlessly excreted in the urine. Proponents of vitamin C supplements believe that 1000 milligrams per day is adequate for the desired antioxidant effect. A 2008 study quantified the ability of 1000mg/day of vitamin C to clean up the free radicals in muscle after exercise, but as we noted above, there are questions as to whether this is actually beneficial.

Everything considered, I continue to recommend, and use, daily oral supplements of 1000 milligrams of vitamin C.

Vitamin C has also been shown to be a powerful antioxidant when applied to the skin. This is where real progress is being made. Free radicals derived from metabolic processes interfere with the production and maintenance of collagen in the skin. When collagen fibers are inadequate in number, or misaligned, the skin structure breaks down and loss of elasticity and wrinkling result. Vitamin C protects the skin's collagen, and is necessary for new collagen production and wound healing. Free radicals from the environment have also been said to enter the skin and cause internal tissue damage, though how this occurs is a mystery to me. The function of the skin is to keep the outside environment outside. That's how it works. In fact, the difficulty in getting topical vitamin C, a water soluble vitamin, into the skin illustrates the efficiency of the skin as a barrier. Mechanism aside, topically applied vitamin C works if it can penetrate the skin in sufficient quantities. We will deal with this issue in depth a bit later in the text.

Vitamin E: Along with the knowledge of the destructive capability of free radicals is the knowledge that they are products of normal metabolism and are neutralized by antioxidants. These antioxidants are either endogenous enzymes produced by the body or exogenous antioxidants, derived from the diet. The diet-derived group includes vitamin E (tocopherol), vitamin C (ascorbic acid), carotenes (vitamin A), and many others. Vitamins C and E are among the major nonenzymatic antioxidants active in protecting the skin from the adverse effects of aging and sun damage. For this purpose, topical application seems far more effective than oral supplements. We don't yet know how much is optimal for this function, but we are discovering how to most effectively deliver it to the skin. The fat-soluble vitamin E molecule is too large to fully penetrate the skin in quantities large enough to significantly raise blood levels. But application of vitamin E to the skin has consistently shown the ability to retard the inflammation from sun exposure and UVB damage and, to some extent, reverse the sun damage. There is also a great deal of evidence that the antioxidant activity of vitamins C and E are greatly enhanced when applied together. Current conservative advice is that a diet rich in fruit and vegetables should be adequate for normal healthy adults.

The effect of vitamin E on the skin is another matter. All evidence indicates that it is an important element for maintaining youthful, healthy skin. Topical antioxidants like vitamins C and E are potent tools for preventing and reversing sun damage to the skin. No one doubts their value; the issue is getting the large molecules through the skin, and a great deal of progress has been made on this front. Effective vitamin C serums are generally available, and they work. But delivering enough of the antioxidant remains a problem; measuring its effectiveness objectively is another.

Since sunburn is free radical damage to the skin, a relatively easy way to document the properties of topical antioxidants is to demonstrate their ability to prevent redness from sun exposure. It turns out that both vitamins C and E reduce the red inflammatory reaction from the sun when applied half an hour before exposure. This can be documented and crudely quantified, so we have a way of measuring results and comparing them. When C and E are applied together the effect is cumulative, in other words, more effective than either alone. When another antioxidant, melatonin, is added to C and E, the protective effect is far greater than using C or E alone, or just C and E in combination. Apparently, the addition of melatonin eases the entry of the antioxidants into the skin. This breakthrough has made the topical delivery of antioxidants into the skin a more effective reality. The unique quality of the combined antioxidants has been known for a number of years. Whether the reduced inflammatory response translates to fewer skin cancers is not yet clear. What is known is that vitamins C and E, combined with melatonin, make more of the antioxidant activity available to the skin. And these same antioxidants have been shown to protect the skin from the inflammatory response to the sun and help reverse previous sun damage to the skin. The conclusion that vitamins C, E, and melatonin should be used together is obvious.

Melatonin is produced by the pineal gland in the brain and is known to influence the circadian rhythms of the body: sleeping at night, being awake during the day. Melatonin has also been recognized as among the most powerful of antioxidants. The ability of melatonin to eliminate free-radical contamination in cellular function has been repeatedly demonstrated. And as noted above, it is very effective as a topical antioxidant and for its synergetic action with vitamins C and E. The ability of melatonin to help drive vitamin C into the skin and its anti-inflammatory action make it a very important ingredient in skin-care products. I believe the combination of vitamin C, vitamin E, and melatonin represents the most truly effective way to get enough of these antioxidants into the skin to impede collagen destruction, encourage collagen production, reduce facial wrinkles and undo sun damage.

With this in mind, I spent quite a bit of time developing an antioxidant serum containing potent levels of vitamins C and E and melatonin. It is called Youth Corridor Ultimate C Boost Serum, and it has proven exceedingly effective for patients of all ages and skin types. I truly believe it is the best antioxidant serum available…anywhere, though I do admit to some pride of authorship. More about Antioxidant Boost in the chapter on skin care.

Daily oral supplements of vitamin E have long been recommended, but have fallen into scientific disfavor due to conflicting reports. Some studies claim it promotes cardiac health; others contradict the findings. A 2009 study indicated that most basic studies were universally flawed and suggested that larger (and perhaps larger than tolerated) doses might be necessary to be effective. Most experts no longer encourage taking oral vitamin E supplements until more information is available. Topical use is another matter.

Natural antioxidants and antioxidant supplements: There are many antioxidant supplements available. Most of these compounds have beneficial properties in their natural state. But the question is whether antioxidant *supplements* actually provide the help they promise. Systemic antioxidants are necessary to prevent the oxidation of LDL (bad) cholesterol, which can then become layered into artery walls as life-threatening plaque. In 2009, the American Heart Association declined to underwrite the use of antioxidant supplements for this purpose. It concluded that there is not enough evidence that vitamins C or E or beta-carotene supplements are of any benefit in preventing coronary artery disease, although the report did encourage the dietary intake of foods high in antioxidants in the natural state. Foods such as citrus fruits, carrots, and pomegranates are high on the long list of healthy sources. Green tea is a great source of the powerful antioxidant group called catechins. Catechins have been credited with improving cardiac health, among other benefits, and many experts encourage consuming multiple cups of green tea daily. Numerous studies show the benefit of these catechins in boosting immune response and protecting against cancer. Green tea extract applied to the skin is active in protecting against skin cancers caused by UVB rays, the most dangerous wavelength in sunlight. There appears to be enormous value in consumption of green tea and its use in skin-care preparations. Here the question is how much intake is necessary to achieve a significant beneficial effect.

Decaffeinated tea retains its antioxidant value as well, so you can drink your antioxidant all day, buzz-free. Green tea is not baked in the production process and maintains more of its active catechins than other types of teas. Green tea has no calories, and though it is admittedly an acquired taste, once you get into it, it tastes great.

Becoming a serious green tea drinker, one should be cognizant of the importance of not drinking scalding liquids for the injury they might cause. A 2016 WHO study established a statistical link between drinking beverages above 149 degrees Fahrenheit and oral and esophageal cancer. Most Americans do not drink beverages at so high a temperature, and properly prepared Japanese green tea is not meant to be served scalding. If it is uncomfortable to drink it is too hot.

Lycopene is a very potent dietary antioxidant. It is found in abundant supply in tomatoes, carrots, and other yellow, red, and orange fruits and vegetables. Its importance in cardiovascular health has been established, and one can infer that if it gets into the arteries it will also reach the skin. There is also some evidence that dietary lycopene protects against some forms of cancer, particularly prostate cancer, but this is far from a hard fact. Here's the good news about lycopene: It appears to be most effective in the cooked state in tomatoes, and is most readily digested and absorbed in combination with fats such as olive oil and cheese. Which makes an excellent case for pizza.

Coldwater fish, like salmon, herring, and mackerel, supply abundant amounts of healthy omega-3 fatty acids, while supplements may not. This does not mean that supplements do not help, simply that there is no evidence of that help. That is not the same thing. In the case of beta-carotene supplements, there is evidence of significant negative impact of high doses on the survival of some cancer and cardiac patients. Based on analysis of major studies the Cleveland Clinic advises against the use of beta carotene supplements, and finds no evidence that vitamin E supplements reduce cardiac mortality.

The point of all this is, don't let faddists fool you. There is no clear, scientific evidence that supplements can do the same job as healthy eating. So, why do I continue to use, and suggest the use of, vitamin C supplements? The evidence of its effectiveness comes and goes in waves. There is nothing to indicate vitamin C is harmful, and reputable scientific investigators have taken both sides of the question over the years. But one would not be wrong in abandoning vitamin C supplements as well.

10. Get the facts about hormone replacement therapy.

Hormones are integrally involved with the overall state of bodily functions. Diseases excluded, there are changes in certain hormone levels that are predictably associated with aging. Just as testosterone and human growth hormone levels decrease in the aging male, so estrogen levels in females dip slowly through adult life, finally reaching symptomatic levels at menopause. The importance of estrogen is well known beyond hot flashes and loss of childbearing ability. The incidence of heart disease in postmenopausal women nearly equals that of men of the same age, in sharp contrast to the very low incidence of heart disease in premenopausal women. Consequently, it has long been thought that estrogen is profoundly protective effect against heart disease, but the latest information strongly refutes this theory. Yet the fact is that coronary artery disease occurs about a decade later in life in women than it does in men, leading to the assumption that the disappearance of estrogen may play a role.

There does seem to be unanimity in believing hormone replacement therapy is effective against loss of bone density. Estrogen withdrawal is followed rapidly by skin changes. Dryness, marked wrinkling, and loss of skin quality are the hallmarks. These are but three of the changes, but they are striking and important to consider. They are preventable, and perhaps reversible, with estrogen therapy. Unfortunately, that is only half of a complicated and incomplete story.

Hormone replacement therapy is known to increase the risk of uterine cancer. In women who have undergone hysterectomy and therefore have no uterus, the risk of uterine cancer is absent and estrogen replacement therapy had been routinely suggested for its alleged cardiovascular protective effects and skin-salvaging qualities. The overwhelming preponderance of women undergo natural menopause and therefore incur increased risk of uterine cancer with estrogen therapy alone or estrogen-progesterone combination therapy. The best evidence is that estrogen therapy may increase the risk of breast cancer as well. All this was announced in July 2002, when the largest ongoing study of the estrogen replacement issue was stopped because the evidence against estrogen use was so overwhelming that it was deemed too much of a risk to continue.

Current thinking seems to have softened, and further complicated a confusing situation. A 2012 Danish study concluded that hormone replacement therapy does not increase the risk of cardiovascular disease or breast cancer. Other studies disagree. Yet other studies point to HRT for five years, beginning at menopause, as having salutary health benefits and little risk. The jury is out on longer-term replacement therapy.

Hormone replacement therapy is an important, and evolving, matter far beyond the scope of this book, and should be discussed with your doctor.

THINK ABOUT WHAT YOU DO

After you have had time to digest the importance of these general concepts, you will be able to benefit greatly by incorporating them into your own life. If you are reading this book with your elbow on your desk, your cheek cradled in your hand, you are passively stretching the skin of your cheek. The same applies to telephone time. It may not seem like a big deal, but it adds up to repeated, inadvertent fatiguing of the elastic fibers, and it definitely takes its toll. Ultimately, loss of skin elasticity is accelerated. It doesn't happen overnight, but it happens.

If you are saying, "I don't sit with my cheek in my hand," that's just one example, and you are missing the point. Think of similar situations that might apply to you. Do you habitually pull at the skin of your neck? Lots of people do, and you can guess where it leads. How about constantly making that quizzical look with your eyebrows. What do you think causes those vertical frown lines between your eyebrows? Are you one whose eyelids swell when you drink red wine or eat spicy foods? Enough stretching and swelling will result in damage to the delicate skin of the lids, and permanent stretching and looseness will result. How much of this is necessary to cause damage is impossible to quantify. It would be difficult to find human volunteers willing to have their skin stretched out of shape in the name of science.

Suffice it to say, the process of aging and loss of elasticity will be accelerated. Think about it, and try to use common sense in your lifestyle decisions. Changing these unimportant habits is not terribly painful. A spicy meal, a few pulls on the skin, and occasional cheek-cradling are not going to change your life, but make a point of thinking about what you do. Change your habits; reduce the insults to your skin. Nothing here requires the soul of a zealot or the self-denial of a Buddhist monk. Simply make an effort not to make things worse.

SIX

The Self-Help Tools You Need to Know About

I n the best of all possible worlds, the ultimate goal of this effort would be to teach people how to remain their youthful best throughout life. Unfortunately, only a small portion of those who will read this book are young enough to learn to influence the process *before* the signs of aging appear. But for most people it is the visible changes of aging that precipitate action. That means helping those with visible signs of aging, early or late, to intercede, reset the clock, and start again.

Toward this end, you will soon learn effective strategies for dealing with a wide range of problems, many of which require no medical care. We have touched upon some basic do's and don'ts to help make everyday life work for us, not against us. Now we must consider actually making specific efforts to help ourselves. The easiest, and most logical, place to start is the world of skin care and treatment. Originally, skin care and treatment were two distinct worlds. But so much overlap currently exists that separation is no longer productive, and I will move from one to the other as the topic dictates.

This section will cover effective, over-the-counter skin-care products; those products available without prescription. Whenever possible, I will omit trade names and stick to functional grouping and active ingredients, but in some cases it is simply easier to communicate using the names you know. Youth Corridor skin care products embody what I think crucial to help you help yourself, and these will be referred to by name. In some instances I will mention other trade names, and often the availability of competing products, and products that work well within the Youth Corridor strategy.

Youth Corridor products contain no emollients, or surfactants; which pollute water and dissolve necessary, protective natural oils. And all are fragrance and paraben free.

I consider three of the Youth Corridor products therapeutic because they are proactive, producing positive therapeutic changes in the skin biology and appearance. They are *Ultimate Antioxidant C Boost*, *Retinultimate Gel*, and *Youth Corridor No Peel Peel*. I believe they stand uniquely alone in the marketplace. The other Youth Corridor products are excellent, functional, and necessary, and they work synergistically with the therapeutic products. All are at least the equal of excellent products from other manufacturers. Just as I will not hesitate to call nonsense nonsense, I will make every effort to present Youth Corridor products and services honestly. Many of the products you are now using are perfectly suited to their tasks. Often, I encourage my patients to begin using *Youth Corridor Ultimate Antioxidant C Boost*, and *Retinultimate*, and stick with the moisturizer and other basic products that they have been using. If a product is effective for you, use it.

The advertising pages of fashion magazines and the skin-care sections of stores provide a virtual assault of promises and claims. Surprisingly enough, some of these claims are true, which was not always the case. Today's skin-care world is a far cry from the old days, when skin-care lines offered more hope than help. Unfortunately, you mustn't let your guard down; numerous useless additives and false promises still abound, and a trace of some berry or green tea is virtually worthless. But generally things have changed significantly for the better, and there are many truly effective brands are on the market. You should make yourself aware of the active ingredients that are responsible for the efficacy of your favorite products.

ALPHA AND BETA HYDROXY ACIDS

Alpha hydroxy acids are effective exfoliants and have assumed a prominent place in skin-care programs. As exfoliants they encourage the shedding of old cells on the skin's surface and encourage production of new cells. This has the effect of making skin smoother and more youthful. AHAs that penetrate into the dermis of the skin also encourage collagen growth. This function is related to molecule size. AHAs are an effective class of skin peeling agents for both their exfoliating and collagen stimulating abilities. AHAs are part of a routine to get your skin to natural ground zero and prepare it for treatment.

Alpha hydroxy acids are derived from naturally occurring substances, such as sugarcane, milk, and citrus, and are known as glycolic acid, lactic acid, or citric acid, depending on the source. The active ingredients are organic chemical structures called alpha hydroxy acids, hence the generic term. Although there is little difference in mode of activity between the various alpha hydroxy acids, glycolic acid has the smallest molecular size and therefore penetrates the skin more effectively than the others; therefore, it has become the AHA of choice. Used properly, all AHAs can produce good cosmetic results. The secret is in the balance between effects and side effects. We all strive to achieve the exfoliation and collagen building effects of AHA, without the irritating side effects such as flaking skin and irritation. More about that later.

Innumerable alpha hydroxy acids have come and gone as cosmetic companies look for ways to make their products stand out from the others. Sugar, berries, leaves, milk—it really makes little difference; they all work. Again, it's all about the molecular size and the concentration of the AHA. Most over-the-counter products contain up to 10-percent concentration of alpha hydroxy acid. The concentration is not strictly dictated, but manufacturers wisely keep the level low enough to prevent irritation. These preparations, while not regulated by the FDA, must adhere to the "do no harm" rule. In the next step up, aestheticians use a 20-30 percent and even 50-percent concentration, which is more irritating and creates a controlled peel of the dead cells on the surface of the skin, and several days of flaking. Plastic surgeons and dermatologists use up to 70-percent concentrations of AHA, which is very effective in resurfacing the skin but traditionally resulted in days to weeks of redness—not something one should try at home.

Youth Corridor No Peel Peel is a game changing exception. It is a 70% glycolic acid peel incorporating a unique ingredient that dramatically reduces discomfort, irritation and actual peeling of skin. Dead cells are shed, and the peel penetrates effectively, but the absence of irritation makes it painless, and patients return to work immediately with improved skin texture and color. I did not develop this wonderful peel, but we have been so successful using it that it has become a leading Youth Corridor product, and is available through your dermatologist, plastic surgeon, or esthetician. There is also a 50% concentration version of the *Youth Corridor No Peel Peel* for home use. Our clinic suggests a minimum of three peels, at least two weeks apart, followed by home treatments. We usually precede the first peel with manual dermaplaning, to help remove dead cells and prepare the skin for better peel results. The *No Peel Peel* represents an enormous step forward in the pantheon of AHA peels.

The over-the-counter products containing AHAs…not peels…are slow but safe. They do their job, and can be a useful part of a daily routine. Essentials of the alpha hydroxy acid story are these: low-concentration AHA products, like moisturizers with AHA, are effective in improving the appearance of the skin. Various formulations containing from 2-percent to 10-percent AHA are available in many excellent product lines. They shedding of the superficial, keratinized layer of the skin is invisible, and results in a more regular skin surface; it lightens blemishes, and improves very superficial wrinkles and sun damage. At this strength, it will not tighten the skin or eliminate wrinkles, but long-term use offers significant improvement in the overall look of the skin. That is why many products, including moisturizers and eye creams contain low concentration AHA.

Centuries old anecdotes have Cleopatra, Queen of Egypt, bathing in the milk of 700 donkeys, and regularly slathering her skin with wine. Her beauty treatments were therefore lactic acid baths derived from milk, and tartaric acid and resveratrol from grapes. If it worked for Cleopatra, in 50 B.C., what took us so long to catch up?

But don't confuse the use of this low-concentration AHA with the therapeutic AHA peels described above. The regular use of AHA at home over a period of months will improve the look of your skin. The medical application of a series of 70-percent AHA peels will eliminate many superficial wrinkles, smooth the skin, truly reverse visible sun damage and discoloration, and may actually improve the underlying collagen and elastic tissues.

The over-the-counter AHA products are best used daily, over a period of at least several months. The frequency of use should increase with age and need. Continual daily use has been very well tolerated over many years, though I do believe a rest period is useful. Often I suggest use for three weeks of every month. The least concentrated preparations are most suitable for daily use. Extended application is important, but so is the rest period. Jump starting the process with a professional AHA peel helps a lot.

Because daily application seems effective doesn't mean that twice-daily application is better. AHAs are irritants and work by dislodging, or exfoliating, the superficial layer of the skin and encouraging a more rapid cell turnover. A frequent complaint is excessive redness and irritation. If you are lucky enough to avoid this problem with normal use, don't look for trouble. The skin needs time for repair. Even if your skin responds perfectly, alternating periods of use and rest is advisable. Some suggest the younger person use AHA preparations every night for six months, followed by a month without treatment. Most people respond better to three weeks on, one week off, all year, and this routine seems more easily adhered to. Frequency of use and concentration are increased for older people and those with more damaged skin.

For most people the dilute acids aren't effective enough, and a series of more concentrated AHA peels must be performed by a professional to get the process going. Our experience with the 70% *No Peel Peel* has borne this out. These are followed, again, by the long-term, home use of the milder solutions.

Daily use products containing low concentrations of AHA work slowly, but they work. There is no reason not to use them. They help. Some manufacturers say the choice of AHA in cream, gel, lotion, or dilute wash form should be based on the oil level of the skin. Too many choices confuse the issue. Let's keep it simple. To point yourself in the right direction, consider this: The maintenance product provided by your dermatologist or plastic surgeon for use after concentrated alpha hydroxy acid peels is of about the same strength as the over-the-counter products and is not altered for skin type. Sure, there might be the individual whose skin becomes excessively dry from an AHA, but a moisturizer corrects that problem. We find that either the product is tolerated or it is not. If you don't love the product, dump it. There are a great many excellent products available, and one of them—in fact, most of them—will suit you well.

Salicylic acid is a fat-soluble, beta hydroxy acid and an excellent exfoliant, and is useful for its ability to penetrate near oil glands. It is the only clinically popular BHA, and because of its ability to penetrate sebaceous glands, it has long been popular in the treatment of acne. It also serves to clean and reduce the size of the outlet of these glands on the skin, commonly known as pores.

The use of dilute AHA and BHA should not be reserved solely for visible signs of aging. Periodic use for teenage and young adult skin helps remove debris, alleviate blackheads and whiteheads, smooth irregular areas, and reduce pore size. This is one of the primary applications for BHAs like salicylic acid. Women in their twenties and thirties will see a smoothing, clearing effect and long-term benefits from early treatment.

Is it possible that early treatment with AHA and BHA will help prevent or forestall aging of the facial skin? It looks that way. What we do know is that the skin surface improves with use, blemishes fade, and the collagen layer of the skin is enhanced. We haven't been at this long enough to say much else. Can there be negative effects from long-term AHA use? Anything is possible, but after decades of use there has been no significant evidence of risk. Studies continue and the FDA surely keeps an eye on it, but so far all reports are positive. Regular use of alpha hydroxy acids and beta hydroxy acids appears beneficial for young and old alike. It will be fascinating to watch the long-term effect of this treatment on people who start at age twenty-five and continue use for decades. Will their skin defy normal aging? How much better will they fare than their peers who did nothing until the signs of aging became undeniable? Will the addition of potent antioxidant therapy make it all a reality? Meanwhile, at age twenty-five or sixty-five, this should become part of your routine.

MOISTURIZERS

A moisturizer is any substance that can force the cells of the superficial keratinized layer of the skin to retain water. These cells are no longer functioning and are in the process of drying and flaking away. These are the same cells that exfoliants, like AHAs, help remove from the surface so that plump, new cells can take their place. If the old cells are not rubbed away to allow the new cells beneath them to be moisturized they leave the skin with a dry, irregular, and superficially wrinkled surface.

Applying water and sealing it in with a moisturizer hydrates and enlarges these superficial cells, thus obliterating the wrinkled, irregular surface and making the skin appear temporarily healthier. There is nothing the least bit healthier about moisturized skin, but it does look better, and that's quite a lot for what little goes into the process.

Most moisturizers are either petroleum-based or water-based. The first ingredient on the label indicates the category. They both work, though the oil-based products are often more effective, if less elegant to the touch. A simple, familiar example is Vaseline, which is very occlusive and holds in moisture. The issue is the elegance of the product, how it feels and how it looks. Most people choose among the well-formulated creams readily available at cosmetic counters. Here the confusion begins. Collagen, hyaluronic acid, seawater, algae, berries, no berries, no collagen? What, no special secret ingredient? That is all beside the point as far as moisturizing potential is concerned. Collagen in a cream does not get into your skin. Period. If you like the product, use it—but not because it contains collagen. The same is true for virtually any special ingredient, the exception being moisturizer/sunscreens, which are what they say they are. Adding treatment ingredients other than pleasant antioxidants to moisture creams seems to defeat the purpose of soothing and moisturizing the skin.

Some moisturizers contain alpha hydroxy acids. This somewhat complicates a simple plan. You should stick to the purest products. Use alpha hydroxy acids as they were intended, as exfoliants. The acid can be delivered in many forms. It is an irritant, so use a moisturizer AFTER application to sooth the skin. The reasoning behind combining AHA with moisturizers is simplification (and marketing) and, to some extent, it works. But it is important to have a simple, pure moisturizer as well. Sometimes your skin needs a break from treatment.

Moisturizers are designed for twice-daily use. They are applied to moist skin and gently rubbed in. There should be no residue, and makeup can be applied directly over them. In some climates and situations, more frequent use is necessary. Any therapeutic skin care products, like vitamin C serum, or retinoids, should always be applied *before* the moisturizer. Obviously, this is so that the active product can be in contact with clean skin. The interface of moisturizer before application would render the therapeutic product useless. A therapeutic product cannot help your skin if it doesn't come in contact with your skin.

One of the bywords in skin-care products these days is "paraben free." Moisturizers, too, are available in paraben-free formulations. Paraben is a preservative, and the addition of preservatives increases the shelf life of the product well beyond the length of time necessary for consumption. It makes life easier for manufacturers and merchants, but though it does nothing for the user, there is no significant evidence linking paraben with harmful side effects in humans. It seems safe enough, but has been virtually banished based on baseless interpretation of questionable data perpetuated by people with a little bit of knowledge. But if products can be made without paraben, little is sacrificed, and why do battle for no good reason? Most good skin-care lines, including all the Youth Corridor products, are paraben free. There are too many good moisturizers to list. Prices vary widely, as do ingredients and one's personal taste. Find a moisturizer that you like and use it.

Youth Corridor Ultimate Moisture Crème is an effective, especially rich moisturizer, designed for use after *Retinultimate* gel and *Ultimate C Boost* serum. It contains ectoin, a biological moisture retaining substance, and is surfactant/emulsifier free, so it doesn't destroy the protective basal moisture layer. We think that is a big plus. That aside, if your moisturizer fits your lifestyle and pocketbook, there is no pressing reason to change.

SUNSCREENS

In otherwise normal, healthy people, there are two primary external causes for accelerated aging of the skin: sun exposure and cigarette smoking. It's as simple as that. No hedging, no modifying, no softening the blow.

Sun exposure activates free radicals within the skin, and sets up an oxidative process in which collage is denatured, thinning the skin and causing wrinkles. It disturbs normal pigmentation, resulting in dark spots, creates surface irregularities, and promotes mutations in cells, which can lead to skin cancer.

Innumerable studies have reinforced what most physicians already knew: The majority of undesirable clinical features associated with accelerated skin aging are the result of damage due to ultraviolet radiation. That means basically sunlight, and excludes X-rays and other forms of radiation. Ultraviolet light is divided into groups based on the wavelength of the light. We are concerned primarily with the bands of light called ultraviolet A and ultraviolet B (UVA and UVB). They are closely related, and the spectrum of one melds into the spectrum of the other. UVA is much more prevalent in the environment, but a thousand times less effective at causing serious skin injury. UVA is associated primarily with skin aging, but increasingly, it has been indicted in skin cancers, including melanoma.

There is less UVB radiation in the atmosphere, but it is more generally destructive. UVB is responsible for the majority of sunburn, skin cancer, and causes skin aging as well. Therefore, we must protect against both. UVB radiation is largely absorbed by the ozone layer of the atmosphere. As the ozone layer has become depleted due to chronic pollution, the incidence of skin cancer has risen proportionally. The accelerated skin aging from UVB exposure is not as easily measured as the numbers of skin cancers per year, but since the same insult stimulates both processes, it too must be affected. Although both UVA and UVB contribute to burning, aging, and skin cancers, an easy way to remember which is which is: UVA=aging, UVB=burning.

Exposure to the sun causes a whole range of reactions. Some are immediately detectable and predictable. There is an immediate inflammatory, or reddening, phase followed by burning in some people and tanning in others. Gradual exposure to the sun affords protection from burning in many individuals, particularly those with darker skin. This ability to tan varies from person to person but can be traced ultimately to one's genetic origins. As a rule, fair-skinned Northern Europeans suffer sunburn, while those of southern ancestry tend to tan. At the other end of the spectrum, the skin pigment of individuals of African descent provides the most effective protection. All this is, of course, a rough generalization. We are no longer purebred anything, and we must learn our own reaction to the sun by trial and error. Those with more pigment or greater tanning ability are more tolerant of the sun, and the tan itself offers some measure of protection from some, but not all, of the harmful effects of ultraviolet radiation. African Americans must protect their skin as well. The incidence of actual sunburn is reduced, but no one is exempt from long-term sun damage. Sun-damaged skin, whether through tanning or burning, shows characteristic changes under the microscope. They are primarily degenerative changes within the collagen layer that result in loss of elasticity and wrinkling. The outer, epidermal layer becomes hyperactive, thickening and causing irregularities and blotchy discoloration on the skin. All together, this coarse leathery, blotchy, wrinkled skin is called prematurely aged. The changes under the microscope are specific and can be clearly distinguished from the normal skin of an older individual. This is something clearly destructive that we are responsible for doing to ourselves. It is unnecessary, and it is avoidable.

The most critical change due to sun exposure is greatly increased susceptibility to skin cancer. I have chosen the word *susceptibility* intentionally. There is no doubting the relationship of sun to skin cancer, and there is now some evidence that chronic sun exposure depresses the immune system and weakens the defenses against skin cancer. Aging of the skin and skin cancer are so closely related to sun exposure that one can hardly think of one without the other.

In 2015, The American Cancer Society estimated that 5.4 million new skin cancers will be diagnosed each year. The most common causative factor is UVB radiation…sunlight. Some eighty percent of these will be basal cell carcinomas; they are the most easily cured of all cancers. Basal cell carcinomas rarely metastasize and are usually not a significant health hazard, though they must be removed before they enlarge, change in nature, or destroy surrounding structures.

Squamous cell carcinoma accounts for about 16% of skin cancers, also caused by sun exposure, and more dangerous than basal cell carcinomas. The least numerous of these skin cancers is melanoma. Approximately 100,000 of these potentially lethal lesions will arise this year. Until not too long ago, a causal relationship hadn't been established between sun exposure and melanoma. Current theory is that actual sunburn, not tanning, predisposes an area of skin to melanoma. UVA radiation, the supposed less-dangerous band length, has been singled out as the causative agent. UVA is the predominant band of the ultraviolet light spectrum used in tanning salons, so draw your own conclusions about that. But UVB is usually cited as the primary stimulus for the cellular mutations responsible for non-melanoma skin cancers. The issue is becoming increasingly unclear. *The Journal of the National Cancer Institute* published a study indicating that people with sun-damaged skin had lower incidence of melanoma, suggesting protection by sunlight-induced pigment. Others point out that a high preponderance of melanomas arise on parts of the body "where the sun don't shine," meaning areas covered by clothing. Fair-skinned, blue-eyed people are the most likely candidates to develop melanoma, those with darker skin the least. In darker-skinned individuals, melanomas frequently develop on the palms, soles of the feet, and under the fingernails. Melanoma is a dangerous disease that is treated aggressively, and the truth is, we do not know enough about its relationship to sun exposure. The good news about melanoma has been its responsiveness to immunotherapy, offering hope in previously hopeless situations.

If all this talk of skin cancer and accelerated aging seems frightening, it is meant to be. Think about this: Eighty percent of a person's ultraviolet (sun) exposure is accumulated before age eighteen. And yet most skin cancers are a disease of middle age and older. Sun damage is a cumulative phenomenon. We pay for our sins long after the day at the beach. An old study from Harvard Medical School estimated that the use of effective sunscreen during the first eighteen years of life would reduce the level of non-melanoma skin cancers by seventy-eight percent—a very impressive number indeed. If you are fair skinned, then for no other reason than cancer protection you must become a devoted user of sunscreen and protective clothing if you enjoy any outdoor activities.

Sun exposure is also the primary culprit in premature aging of the skin. That cannot be said often enough. Decades of scientific study have established an irrefutable cause-and-effect relationship; we must decide how to manage the facts. There is no reason to deny yourself the enjoyment of the great outdoors. Nor is there reason to so restrict your lifestyle that the slightest tan becomes a source of concern. That is simply too extreme, and, as we all know, some sunlight is necessary for the skin to produce vitamin D. However, you must protect yourself where you can. It does not make sense to sunbathe, and certainly not without adequate protection. You can learn to enjoy the regenerating feel of the sun without doing harm. It is not a terribly restricting concept. Wide-brimmed hats, sunscreen and common sense are here to stay.

There are two categories of sunscreens that you need to know about: physical and chemical sunscreens. The former are like zinc oxide—the white stuff the lifeguards put on their noses—and do their job by acting as a physical barrier to the sun. These are effective at reflecting light, thereby protecting the skin. Titanium dioxide, a finer and therefore a bit less noticeable than zinc oxide, is the other regularly used physical sunblock. Both are very effective at protecting the skin from UVA and UVB rays. Titanium dioxide and zinc oxide have been incorporated into more manageable compounds and are less visible while remaining an excellent block. The physical blocks seem to dissipate more easily in water than do chemical sunscreens.

Chemical sunscreens absorb ultraviolet radiation as filters. Various chemicals protect against the spectrum of ultraviolet light. The oldest and formerly most commonly used of these was para-aminobenzoic acid (PABA). Pure PABA use has almost disappeared due to the high incidence of allergy and irritation associated with it. There is also some evidence that use of PABA may cause DNA damage. The only PABA formulation permitted for use in America is padimate O. Other compounds have taken up the slack. Excellent, frequently used UVB screens include octinoxate and other cinnamates, and benzophenone. Oxybenzone and avobenzone (Parsol 1789) screen out UVA radiation. These compounds are very effective, and if you pick up the sunscreen you currently use, you will find some of them listed among the ingredients. The package should also be clearly marked with the sun protection factor (SPF) of the product. The SPF refers to the laboratory-determined time required for skin to burn with sunscreen as opposed to the time required for the same level of sunburn without protection. A sunscreen that offers an SPF of 2 would allow an individual who would burn in ten minutes to be exposed to the sun for twenty minutes before reaching the same level of sunburn. Similarly, SPF 15 products should allow the same individual one hundred fifty minutes of safe exposure. Does one application of SPF 15 really afford you more than two hours of protection? In theory, yes; in reality, no. It depends on how quickly you would burn without sunscreen, the conditions at the moment, how well and how thickly the sunscreen was applied, and whether it had been rubbed, washed or sweated off. More importantly, sun damage is not limited to burning. Accelerated aging and skin cancers can result without burning. UVA is not screened out by normal glass partitions, so skin aging continues. And most cotton clothing is ineffective as a sunblock, so don't count on it. Wet shirts do little to protect you on a sunny beach day, though sun protective clothing is becoming more effective and popular.

The SPF is only a guide. Products with ratings of 30 or higher have become the norm, but even they require repeated application to remain effective. Sunscreens with increasingly high SPF numbers are only marginally more effective than SPF 30. This is where marketing takes over from common sense. Here are the facts: SPF 15 blocks 93 percent of the UVB to which skin is exposed; SPF 30 blocks 97 percent, SPF 50 blocks 98 percent and SPF 100 blocks 99 percent of UVB rays. Hence there is little effective difference between SPF 30 and SPF 100. Several efforts have been made to limit SPF at 50, but so far the forces of the marketplace have won the day. Sun protection products with an SPF of 30 are extremely effective, and have the added benefit of often being more amenable to elegant compounding, and therefore a more pleasant product. The important thing is applying sunscreen liberally twenty to thirty minutes before exposure, replenishing it regularly, at least every hour, preferably more frequently, and after swimming.

A new bit of information about protection is now being factored into our thinking. When antioxidants vitamins C and E and melatonin are applied to the skin thirty minutes before exposure, there is a significant reduction in the sunburn response. These antioxidants appear to have potent anti-inflammatory properties, which protect against sunburn as well as being able to reverse sun damage on the cellular level. This is the reason some sunscreens now contain antioxidants. I encourage our patients to use *Youth Corridor Ultimate Antioxidant C Boost*. It contains a combination of vitamins C, E and melatonin, and daily usage helps protect from, and reverse sun damage. But this is not a substitute for sunscreen, but should be used regularly in the morning for additional protection.

When picking a sunscreen, you should check for these things:

1. SPF. The standard is 30, with broad spectrum protection, meaning UVA and UVB. There is little to be gained by using higher SPF as the protection factor levels off after 30. SPF 30 filters out 97 percent of the sun's rays. SPF 50 filters out 98 percent, and to get this little bit extra, more ingredients are added and the products are often less pleasant to use.

2. Active ingredients. Through trial and error you will eliminate products and ingredients that are unpleasant or irritating to your skin.

3. Water-resistant or waterproof. This is an important consideration for swimming or sports. Water-resistant means that the product continues to protect for up to forty minutes of immersion; waterproof means protection for up to eighty minutes after immersion. In the past these had been thicker or more difficult to spread than other products, but recently they seem to have become more elegant. If you plan to spend time at the beach, they are certainly worth a try.

Many manufacturers now offer combination sunscreen and moisturizer products. This is a useful idea, if only because it simplifies routines and helps make using sunscreen a habit. Two questions arise: (1) Do these formulations work as well and feel as good as moisturizer alone? Only you can make the determination regarding the aesthetic appeal of the product. And: (2) Does one need sunscreen only twice daily, as often as moisturizer is suggested? Probably not. Especially when outdoor time is planned. But surprisingly, the best time to apply sunscreen is before it is necessary, so that it has time to interact with the keratinized (top) layer of the skin. Moisturizer/sunscreen can be applied morning or night. A lot depends on your lifestyle and where you live. Sunny climates and high altitudes require more protection on a daily basis than the bleak north at sea level. So assuming the combination moisturizer/sunscreen is as effective as sunscreen alone, does the combination simplify or complicate your skin-care routine?

It has always seemed to me that the combination products are good primarily because they simplify the number of steps, and make it more difficult to skip sunscreen out of laziness, and we are all lazy. Make using them as much a part of the morning routine as brushing your teeth.

Add more sunscreen as your activities demand.

SEVEN

YOUTH CORRIDOR STRATEGY
A Skin-Care Routine That Works

What can a good skin-care routine do? If you asked that question twenty-five years ago, the answer would have been "very little." Although sunscreens had been available since the 1960s, they weren't efficient or popular until the 1990s. Moisturizers did little more than temporarily rehydrate skin, and there were no effective products to combat free radicals in the skin, encourage collagen growth, reverse sun damage, exfoliate dead cells, encourage cell turnover, or fight wrinkles, blemishes, and brown spots.

Today, your skin-care routine can neutralize destructive environmental and metabolic free radicals; encourage healthy collagen growth; reduce and eliminate fine wrinkles; reverse sun damage; prevent further sun damage; encourage cell turnover; and make skin healthier, clearer, more evenly pigmented and generally more youthful and better looking. That's a lot of progress. It is all possible, and you should not settle for less. Good products are available at most price points, although some of the more complex compounds are a bit pricier. Virtually everyone can afford to help themselves with these products, and the routine takes only minutes morning and evening. This is something positive you can do for yourself with little more than a few simple instructions.

Here is what you will need:

1. A good skin cleanser.
2. Two excellent moisturizers, one with sunscreen and one without.
3. Sunscreen.
4. A preparation with alpha hydroxy acid.
5. A vitamin C serum or, preferably, a vitamin C, E and melatonin antioxidant serum.
6. A retinoid product, or other skin brightener, to even skin tones.
7. Enriched eye-area/thin skin moisture cream containing peptides, antioxidants or AHA.
8. Exfoliating mask.
9. Peeling agent.

Not everyone will need every one of these products. Obviously one does not need a bleaching cream or brightener if skin doesn't have dark patches or under-eye pigment, although these are the most popular products in the Asian market, where sun protection is a religion, and unblemished, light skin is prized.

Routines vary with one's stage in life. For the moment I will generalize. Later in the book, examples will be given that touch on varied ages and problems. You should be able to find your situation among them. If not, you can e-mail one of our skin-care experts at info@youthcorridorclinic.com and we will be happy to help guide you to a proper routine.

CLEANING...CLEANSING...WASHING

A good skin-care routine must make sense, and to work it must be easy to adhere to.

The basic routine applies to everyone. A proper routine should function on several levels and always begins with cleaning, or cleansing, the skin. I still like the word *cleaning*, because it lets one know what has to be done. Either way, it refers to the ability to remove makeup, the daily buildup of environmental grit and free radicals and the constantly produced crop of cellular debris and surface oils. These oils are both fresh and denatured but cannot be readily separated from one another. Optimally, one should remove the oxidized oils and preserve the fresh skin oil, with its natural moisturizing qualities. The basal layer of the epidermis contains a protective lipid layer that plays a role in retaining moisture and the integrity of the skin. If possible, this layer should remain undisturbed. Most soaps and cleansers contain detergent like emulsifiers and surfactants, which facilitate the interface between oil, or lipid, and water. They work by mobilizing and washing away all moisturizing lipid elements, not just the oxidized oil and debris. After removal of the combination of existing one must start fresh. Night and day, removing oxidized oils and free radical debris is good for your skin.

Whatever method you choose, soap, cleanser, or emulsifier-free cleanser, it is imperative that old oil, debris, and makeup be effectively removed before applying skin treatments. As I mentioned previously, for an antioxidant serum, or a skin brightener to work, it must be in contact with the skin surface. Dead cells, old skin oil, and debris, prevent the treatment from going where they need to go: directly onto your skin. It is also important to clean the skin to avoid blocking pores (the microscopic outlet for oil glands) and causing skin irregularities and infection.

In earlier editions of this book I stood firmly in the camp of soap and water to do all of the above, despite the fact that Youth Corridor products included a gentle cleanser that many people loved. The problem with soap and water is twofold. Not only does soap remove debris and denatured skin oils, but it cannot distinguish between denatured lipids and the skin's protective deep layer. And, as every woman knows, soap and water does a poor job of removing makeup.

Soap is a detergent. It works by emulsifying oils and foaming them away, along with surface debris. Even gentle, superfatted soaps work this way. Most women turned to cleansers, which did a better job of removing makeup, unaware that they were still washing away the good oils with the bad.

In developing the newest Youth Corridor products one of our goals was to avoid all emulsifiers and surfactants in our products. Those are the chemicals that make detergents foam, and also pollute waste water. A number of surfactants and emulsifiers found in skin care products, soaps, and detergents have already been targeted for elimination by the California Green Chemistry Initiative. Being ahead of the curve, and environmentally friendly is surely something that made us proud, and we were able to do so while achieving our mission to avoid disturbing the intrinsic lipids of the epidermis. *Youth Corridor Dual Action Cleanser* effectively removes makeup, denatured oils, and debris, but doesn't foam away essential, protective basal oils.

Non-foaming products are the future. I recommend them highly, and believe in them. However…and there's always a however, coming from the old soap and water school, a lifetime of habits are hard to change. Washing with soap and water, and exfoliating by toweling dry, works well, as long as one replenishes lost moisture. Is this as good as using the new, non-foaming cleansers, such as *Youth Corridor Dual Action Cleanser*? No. There is no excuse for removing good oils with the bad; no need for a separate product to remove makeup; and no excuse for polluting the environment. Obviously, women embraced the new, non-foaming technology first. Slow as they are, men are catching on.

ANTIOXIDANTS

After your skin has been cleansed free of denatured oils, and environmental debris, and dead cells, the healthy surface is most receptive to being nurtured, "fed," and treated. The first order of business is neutralizing the free radicals which have accumulated and worked their way into the living cells near the surface and deeper in the collagen producing dermis.

Free radicals sitting idly on the keratinized layer of dead cells are unlikely to do any harm, as they are attacking already dead cells, ready to be shed, and easily cleansed away twice a day. We should consider them nothing more than culprits by association with the destructive free radicals within the skin that cause aging and collagen breakdown. And that is where our efforts must be directed. It is the free radicals produced within the living skin cells of the dermis and basal layer of the epidermis that must be neutralized. In doing this the free radicals remaining on the skin surface are easily treated as well.

Obviously, in order to neutralize these more destructive free radicals within the skin, the neutralizing agents…antioxidants…must penetrate the protective barriers of the skin. That is where the difficulty lies. As I have said repeatedly, the skin serves to keep the inside in, and the outside out. It is a relatively impermeable barrier that protects the homeostasis of our bodies. There are many well-known, naturally occurring antioxidants of varying strengths and effectiveness. Their usefulness in skin care depends largely on their ability to penetrate the skin. A potent antioxidant that remains solely on the skin surface may interface with the dead cells of the superficial cornified layer, but it does nothing to reverse photodamage (sun) or encourage collagen production. To serve you properly an antioxidant must reach the deeper layers of the skin.

For a number of well-documented, scientifically proven reasons, vitamin C may well be the most important of the skin related antioxidants. The active form of vitamin C is L-ascorbic acid. This form is the most difficult to deal with, but simply put, the only truly active, useful, form of vitamin C, and it is necessary for the production of collagen. The word ascorbic literally means "no scurvy" since it is ascorbic acid that is necessary for collagen production and the prevention of the disease, scurvy, in which wounds don't heal for the inability to produce collagen. Vitamin C has also been shown to have both a remarkable sun protective ability, and the ability to reverse sun damage. If that is not enough, vitamin C also lightens skin tones and reverses fine wrinkles by rebuilding and realigning collagen.

All this being the so, the issue is getting vitamin C to penetrate the skin. Here is where I repeat myself, having outlined this in the earlier section on vitamin C, but it is important enough be worth the effort. Vitamin C is a water soluble compound, so it does not easily penetrate the lipid layers of the skin. But in combination with fat soluble substances like vitamin E, it becomes significantly more effective. There are many theories of why this is so, but for our purposes the simple fact that the two vitamins are more effective when used together is sufficient. When I was doing the initial literature survey before formulating *Youth Corridor Antioxidant C Boost*, I came across reports of several studies in which vitamin C was combined with melatonin, yielding more powerful antioxidant protection. A very basic experiment was structured based on the fact that sunburn is a form of free radical damage, and therefore would be prevented by effective antioxidant protection. Skin protected with the topical application of vitamin C became less red after sun exposure that untreated skin. A combination of vitamins C and E resulted in still less redness. But the big surprise was that the addition of melatonin to the C and E resulted in significantly greater sun protection, a measure of the potent antioxidant activity of this unique combination.

That combination, vitamin C, vitamin E, and melatonin became the basis for *Youth Corridor Ultimate Antioxidant C Boost*, which has proved extremely effective in reversing sun damage, reducing wrinkles, lightening and evening skin tone, and building collagen. While it is definitely not a sunscreen, I recommend pre-sun exposure application of *Youth Corridor Antioxidant C Boost* for additional protection against the ageing damage of sun exposure.

There are a number of effective vitamin C serums available, each different in some aspect from the others. The most important fact to remember in choosing an effective vitamin C serum is to look for ascorbic acid as the key active ingredient. All other forms of vitamin C are only marginally effective. The natural question is why any manufacturers would use any form of vitamin C other than pure L-ascorbic acid. The answer is simple; vitamin C esters, and other chemical forms, are far easier and less expensive to produce. Yes, they can legally claim to contain whatever concentration of vitamin C is in the mix, but it doesn't come close to having the antioxidant, collagen building properties of pure L-ascorbic acid.

A bit more of the true science of vitamin C will help make you an expert the next time a poorly informed cosmetic sales person tries to sell you the company line. The optimal concentration of L-ascorbic acid (vitamin C) in a serum appears to be 15%. As the concentration is increased to 20%, and above, the antioxidant activity of the serum decreases. I have found no satisfactory explanation for this phenomenon, but it has been tested and reproduced in independent studies. So the optimal concentration of vitamin C has been established at 15%. *Youth Corridor Ultimate Antioxidant C Boost*, and other good vitamin C serums, make use of this most efficient concentration.

Ascorbic acid is light and oxygen sensitive; therefore, all vitamin C serum containing active ascorbic acid must be packaged in dark-colored glass bottles. That's why you see all those dark brown or blue bottles. In fact, since our treatment line began with *Antioxidant Boost* in a dark blue bottle, it dictated the design of the entire treatment line that grew from it. True ascorbic acid serum has a slightly medicinal odor, which soon dissipates. It's the scent of good things going on, and easily masked by whatever scent you choose.

One last thing about real vitamin C serum. Upon exposure to light and air it begins to take on a yellowish tinge. This is entirely normal. Use your daily dose, and close the bottle tightly. We have titrated the one ounce bottle to be a hundred day supply. As you reach the three month point the serum may turn yellowish. It is still effective. We estimate that at this point it has lost about 10% of its potency through oxidation.

MOISTURIZERS

Once the oil and debris have been cleansed away and active formulations, like vitamin C serum, or retinoids, have been applied, a good routine must provide remoisturization. Moisturizers themselves simply serve to temporarily retain moisture in the superficial layer of the skin. However, after applying treatment products the better moisturizers serve as soothing, calming, agents as well as water retention agents. They are not therapeutic unless other ingredients are added, but they make your skin look and feel good. Moisturizers are usually used twice daily. A good rule of thumb is that moisturizers work for twelve hours. Moisturizing the skin is a fleeting proposition indeed. The actual moisture content of the skin as a whole varies little under normal circumstances. The function of moisturizing compounds is to trap moisture in the superficial skin layer of dead keratinized cells. The nature of this layer varies from dry and scaly to smooth and healthy-looking, depending on the amount of moisture temporarily trapped within. The whole thing is somewhat artificial. On the other hand, the process is mimicking the end point of the natural process. Individuals producing greater amounts of skin oil are, in effect, sealing the moisture into the keratinized layer with their body's own, natural, moisturizer. This substance lasts longer than most moisturizers; but it also oxidizes and traps debris, and must be cleansed away periodically. Surfactant free cleansers are specifically engineered for this purpose, without disturbing the protective basal lipid layer.

For these reasons, we use pleasant, well-tolerated moisture creams and replenish them twice a day—more often, if necessary. You should choose a moisture cream that is soothing, pleasant and simple—one that does not contain active therapeutic ingredients. It is incorrect to think of these ubiquitous creams as treatment, for they do not penetrate the skin or effect any permanent change on the skin surface; nonetheless, they play an important role in the overall plan. Though they have no actual therapeutic value, one cannot deny that they make the skin look and feel better.

Moisturizers won't keep you young; we have other things for that. But moisturizers help seal in the good things you have just done for your skin, and make it look and feel more youthful and beautiful.

This simple routine is easy to follow; it works and it will make a definite and cumulative difference.

ABOUT MOISTURIZERS CONTAINING SUNSCREEN

To quickly go over a topic we have already covered elsewhere, in the best of circumstances, moisturizers containing sunscreen is a good thing. Being generally lazy, it makes sense to use a soothing moisturizer containing sunscreen, thereby eliminating a step in your daily routine and ensuring you daily sun protection. The problem with this strategy has generally been the difficulty in formulating an elegant combination when adding an effective sunscreen to a moisturizer. A small amount of chemical protection is easy to disguise, but trying to reach the magic 30 SPF number is more difficult, particularly if one tries to use physical sunscreens like titanium dioxide or zinc oxide. It is simple enough to produce an elegant SPF 30 sunscreen where the standards for feel and texture are less than demanding, but moisturizers are expected to be elegant, smooth, and inviting to use, which explains why there are few, if any, great moisturizers with full SPF 30 protection. For years our company marketed an SPF 30 sunscreen containing moisturizer. But it is a sunscreen first, and doesn't lend itself to twice daily, year round use.

The Youth Corridor product line currently includes two excellent, elegant, (and expensive) moisturizers. Both are fragrance free, paraben free, and surfactant free. But neither contains sunscreen. They are very soothing moisturizers, designed to be used after *Antioxidant C Boost Serum* and *Retinultimate*, and as all day moisturizing compounds, not as sun protection.

Sunscreens should be used every day by anyone who spends any time at all outdoors. The earlier you begin protection, the younger your skin stays. Simple.

EXFOLIANTS

Exfoliants play an important role in skin care by encouraging the shedding of superficial skin cells. These dead cells cause surface irregularities and detract from the lustrous beauty of even the youngest skin. For the most part, alpha hydroxy acids are the exfoliants of choice. They are effective in reducing surface irregularities as well as brown spots and fine wrinkles, which are the result of photoaging of the skin caused by sun exposure. Alpha hydroxy acids also encourage collagen production and reduce superficial wrinkles. Popular AHAs include glycolic acid, derived from sugar cane, and lactic acid, derived from soured milk. Other AHAs include malic acid, tartaric acid and citric acid. They all work and can be included in your cleanser, moisturizer, or eye cream, or as a stand-alone preparation. In the case of stand-alone AHA creams, the concentration for home care are often as high as 10-percent and may be irritating; therefore, I suggest using them at bedtime followed by soothing moisturizer. But glycolic acid, in combination with other specific ingredients, dramatically reduce the discomfort and irritation associated with glycolic acid and allow the use of significantly more concentrated solutions, with dramatic results. The *Youth Corridor No Peel Peel* is an example. The in-office peel is a 70% solution of glycolic acid. It removes dead cells, encourages collagen production and is neither painful, irritating, nor does it cause peeling and flaking. Dead cells are dissolved away, collagen production is encouraged, and best of all, there is no down time. Using the same formula the 50% glycolic acid home peel is nearly as effective and easy to use. This is an example of the range of concentration of alpha hydroxy acids…from a weak exfoliating agent to an intense peeling agent. The role of AHAs continues to expand in skin care.

Many companies produce AHA masks for exfoliation and a mini-peel. The Youth Corridor mask is a combination of alpha and beta hydroxy acids. The beta hydroxy acid in general use is salicylic acid…aspirin. Its unique property is the ability to penetrate and unclog sebaceous glands. For this reason, it has long been used in the treatment of acne, and in general skin care to reduce pore size. There is definitely a place for beta hydroxy masks in a skin care routine; usually on a weekly basis. Nothing else is as effective in cleaning and reducing pores.

Though routinely helpful, each of these products is specifically useful in combating particular problems. Fine wrinkles and smile lines in the very fine skin around the eyes respond to various retinoids derived from vitamin A as well as antioxidants such as vitamin C, peptides and AHA. Color changes, blotches, and surface irregularities tilt the equation toward looking old and are treated with natural and chemical and botanical bleaching creams and exfoliants. Then, on the deepest level, the routine must do whatever possible to maintain and improve the infrastructure of the skin. Again, antioxidants such as vitamin C are increasingly recognized as being extremely useful. All these functions must be combined in a pleasant, easily learned, rewarding process. No matter how good the routine is, if you don't follow it, it's useless.

NIGHT MOISTURIZER

After application of the nightly active treatments, or any other time during the day, remoisturize your skin. The evening moisturizing step is more for the soothing action of the gentle cream than to enhance appearance. Retin-A and AHAs are irritating; a soothing moisturizing cream will quiet things down.

There are many variables to consider in a skin-care routine, but, special conditions aside, the basic steps apply to everyone. Cleansing, antioxidants, brightening, exfoliating, moisturizing, and sun protection are a must. Individual age-related situations are addressed at the end of the book. At the end of this section, you will see the step-by-step directions for your twice-daily home skin-care routine. This routine alone will make your skin more youthful and attractive. It is the launching pad for other options, but if you do nothing more than these simple steps, you will have made great and visible strides. Healthy skin looks and reacts better. It will stay young longer and even respond to procedures with better results than uncared-for skin. There is no excuse for neglecting this simple exercise in self-help.

GETTING STARTED

Youth Corridor morning skin-care routine

Start by cleaning your skin. If you are in the habit of washing with soap and water in the shower, it isn't the end of the world. But using a modern, effective cleanser is better. *Youth Corridor Dual Action Cleanser* is perfect for the task. If you are happy with your present cleanser, by all means continue using it. Unfortunately, soap is often not up to removing persistent cosmetics; cleansers are better at that. Soap and water are also ineffective at removing makeup, but the bottom line is modern, non-foaming cleanser, traditional cleanser, or soap and water, get your skin clean in the morning.

Most people have mixed areas of oily, dry, and normal skin, with the nose, forehead, and eyebrow area being the oiliest and the cheeks the driest. To complicate matters further, these diverse areas vary in their moisture qualities according to climate. Activities, age, anxiety, stress, hard work, and, especially, sex have a profound effect on oil production and the relative moisture of the skin. As a rule, the skin becomes drier as we age, and accommodations should be made for this on an individual basis. Generally, we cannot predict the state of hydration of the skin from month to month or from hour to hour. It helps our planning to know what we are actually dealing with. To do that, we must return to ground zero. Clean all external substances from the skin surface, use appropriate treatment products, and then seal in moisture with a moisturizer.

Rinse your face with water that feels warm to the touch. It should not actually be hot. Remember that body temperature is 98.6°F. Therefore, any water temperature above that will feel warm. That's all you need. The water must be warm enough to stimulate the blood vessels in the skin to dilate and encourage blood flow. It must also be warm enough to soften skin oils and debris. That will help the cleanser mobilize residual makeup, oxidized skin oils, ambient pollution, and cellular debris from the skin surface.

If you continue to use foaming cleansers or soap, then lather generously with a mild soap or cleanser of slightly acidic pH. The surface of healthy skin has a slightly acidic pH of 5.5, and it makes little sense to upset it. Basis, unscented Dove, and other mild soaps are excellent as far as balance and gentleness are concerned. Avoid heavily perfumed soaps. The pH of some seemingly mild soaps are too basic (alkaline) for the skin, and will leave a residue. Others contain antibacterial formulations, which may be an irritant to certain skin types. The rule of thumb is to choose a brand that feels good, lathers well in your local water, and seems to wash off without leaving residue. Or get modern and use a non-foaming, surfactant free, non-polluting cleanser.

Cleansers are more effective at removing makeup than is soap. Many cleansers are fortified with antioxidants like green tea or AHAs, so they add a little therapeutic action that is beneficial. There are not high enough concentrations of these ingredients in any cleansers to be therapeutic alone, but a little doesn't hurt. Even if you choose to wash your face with soap and water in your morning shower, cleansers should be used at night to remove residual makeup and the debris from the day, and they are generally pleasant to use.

Using cleanser and a soft pad, cloth, or your hands, gently work the cleanser into the skin of the face and neck. Don't forget the eyelids. Get all that old makeup off (which should have been done properly the previous night, but nobody's perfect). This should take only thirty seconds.

Wash the cleanser or lather off with copious amounts of warm water.

Repeat the process. This time, follow the warm-water rinse with a refreshing final rinse with cold water. That will close down the blood vessels and firm the skin, and it feels great.

Toweling off is useful. After washing, use your towel for exfoliation. After showering or washing your face, towel briskly. This should be done at least once a day. The process helps remove heaped-up dead skin cells and allows healthy young cells to reach the surface. Toweling should always be done in the down-to-up direction to avoid stretching the skin downward and helping gravity. Be gentle with yourself. The towel will do a great job with virtually no pressure at all. It feels good, and your skin will assume a healthy glow from even the gentlest contact. Though the glow will retreat rapidly, your skin will look far better for this gentle exfoliation.

Skin treatments and serums should be applied to clean, dry skin. After thorough cleansing, antioxidant serum should be applied. This usually includes vitamins C and E. A few drops of the liquid are spread evenly over the face, taking care to include areas of wrinkling as well as the cheeks and forehead.

I always suggest the use of the vitamin C and E and melatonin antioxidant, *Youth Corridor Ultimate Antioxidant C Serum*, preferably in the morning, to get the extra sun protection during the day, but it can be used before bed as well. It all depends on one's routine, and what therapeutics are being used at night. In either case, it should be applied to clean skin before other products to allow it to penetrate into the skin. Six to eight drops are applied to the skin of the face and neck, and the remainder rubbed onto the back of the hands. Using this measured therapeutic amount daily results in a hundred day supply of *Antioxidant C Boost*. This is calculated to retain potency when the ascorbic acid begins to interact with oxygen. The serum will begin to darken slightly in color over this period, losing up to ten percent of its antioxidant activity by the end of the three month cycle.

Skin brighteners, usually of botanical origin, should be applied next. These products help reduce areas of pigmentation and even out skin tone. They also add a healthy glow. Retinoids, which also act as brightening, lightening agents, in addition to combating wrinkles and enlarged pores, are usually applied at night. Chemical bleaching creams, such as hydroquinone in prescription strength, are usually applied in the evening, as well. If they are applied in the morning, be sure a sunscreen is included in the compound.

I suggest applying only one serious therapeutic agent morning or night. So use a vitamin C serum morning, retinoid at night. Or reverse the order, but one at a time.

Moisturizer. After the morning wash, after smoothing on antioxidant skin serum and/or brightener and before applying makeup, a moisturizer, or a moisturizer containing sunscreen should be applied. This is a routine that works best when it doesn't vary. Surely you will not suffer significant ultraviolet damage to your skin in Chicago in February while commuting by train or auto from home to an indoor workspace. Under those circumstances it would be safe to eliminate the sunscreen step. But when do you begin again—and what about a day outdoors? The only routines that work are those that become routine. When you find a moisture/sunscreen combination that is easily tolerated, use it every day.

If sunscreen is used separately, that's fine too, but you have to use it. No cheating. It should be applied before the moisturizer so it can penetrate. Moisturizers are best applied to moistened skin. The need for moisturizer often varies inversely with the need for sunscreen. That means when the weather is cold and you retreat to the heated indoors, you have little need for sunscreen. The same circumstances are powerful drying influences. Cold air with very low humidity and superheated, dry indoor air desiccate skin and increase the need for moisture treatment. This is a good place to talk about how much cream and lotion is enough. Moisturizers, sunscreens, and treatments should be applied to the skin surface and gently rubbed in. All evidence of the cream should disappear. There should be no surface residue, no slippery, greased feeling. There is no advantage to be gained from using more than the thin layer that disappears readily into the surface of the skin. You should not see it, and it should not feel greasy.

YOUTH CORRIDOR EVENING SKIN-CARE ROUTINE

Evening skin cleansing is generally performed with cotton sponges or cloth and a gentle cleanser, like *Youth Corridor Dual*

Action Cleanser. Non-foaming cleansers need to be thoroughly applied in order to be effective at removing debris and makeup. Foaming cleansers also work well, despite the environmental disadvantages and disruption of the basal lipid layer. Find one that feels good and works for you. Cleansers are far better than soap and water for this task, but if you are happy with one of the superfatted, mild soaps like Dove or Basis, use it. Probably the most important aspect of a facial soap is that it is pH-balanced to the slight acidity of the skin.

After cleansing, apply *Youth Corridor Ultimate Antioxidant C serum*, unless you have decided on the morning application routine. Once a day is enough. Six to eight drops of the serum is applied to the face and neck with the fingertips. The remainder is rubbed into the back of the hands to reverse sun damage and keep the hands looking youthful and healthy.

If vitamin C serum is used in the morning, evening routine should include *Youth Corridor Retinultimate* gel. This is a unique therapeutic product. The gel is smooth and pleasant to the touch, and is easy to use. The retinoid ingredient is a vitamin A derivative, and is related to all retinol products, including tretinoin (Retin A). *Retinultimate* does not require a prescription. It is remarkably non-irritating, and brightens and lightens skin, reduces fine wrinkles, and balances skin tones. *Retinultimate* also has a unique ability to penetrate oil glands, or pores, and prevent or treat acne-type lesions. Its cell turnover and lightening effect is not equal to tretinoin, but neither does it cause redness and dryness of the skin.

For general skin care for the younger patient a brightener is applied in the evening if there are early signs of uneven skin tones. This is applied to all the facial skin, not just the area of blemishes. Brighteners are gentle and slow acting, but definitely make a difference.

If significant dark areas, or melasma, are present prescription products containing hydroquinone can be used to reduce color and even out skin tone. These should only be used on the area in question, and for as long as dark areas persist. If 4-percent hydroquinone is used, it requires prescription and should be monitored by a physician.

Other treatments like 10-percent AHA creams should be applied at night as well. All these treatments should be followed by the application of a soothing moisturizer to counteract the irritant effect they have. Most eye creams fall into this category. They are generally thicker moisturizers with active ingredients like AHA or peptides in fairly high concentration and are best applied at night when makeup has been removed. It is not necessary to follow eye cream with moisturizer. Youth Corridor produces an eye and neck cream for this purpose. The skin of the eyelids and neck are both very thin, delicate, and subject to early wrinkling. The same mild ingredients are effective for both areas, and using a single product simplifies the process.

If you use Tretinoin (Retin-A), the twenty-minute waiting period after washing is annoying, particularly at bedtime. A routine will be much more pleasant and easier to stick to without such restrictions. With the effectiveness of so many retinoid products derived from vitamin A as well as the new antioxidant and AHA products, most people can do quite well without Tretinoin. But it is an excellent product; and if you need it, it is worth the trouble.

There are any number of other products that may play a useful role in a skin care, but the basics are clean, treat, and moisturize. You will protect your skin from early aging, undo damage from sun and the environment, build collagen, and protect against skin cancer. The equation is a simple one, heavily balanced on the plus side, and should be part of daily life for young and old alike.

That's all there is to a good, therapeutic skin-care routine. A few minutes in the morning, a few minutes at night, good products that actually work, and a routine you stick to. Using effective ingredients, you should see an improvement in your skin in ten days, but the commitment is long-term. Your skin will get better and look better, and you will be doing your part to stay in that attractive Youth Corridor.

EIGHT

Tools of the Trade

The following are noninvasive and minimally invasive treatments for specific problems. In the Youth Corridor strategy of Prevention, Maintenance, and Correction, they generally fall under the heading of Maintenance…but there is significant overlap at the margins of the three categories.

We will begin with the most basic of maintenance-correction modalities: AHA peels. Most of the information here has been presented earlier in the book, but in an effort to make most sections work on a stand-alone basis, I will burden you by repeating it.

ALPHA HYDROXY ACID PEELS

Alpha hydroxy acid, AHA, is everywhere. Some preparations call it fruit acid; others combine the names with proprietary products. The active ingredients remain the same. The purpose of the preparations is to exfoliate the dead cell layer of the stratum corneum, encourage growth of new cells, and eliminate superficial wrinkles and discolorations. AHAs have a positive effect on the nature and thickness of collagen as well. The preparations are available in various strengths and are reasonably effective. What is produced is a superficial peel, without the associated side effects and possible complications of deep peels, such as trichloric acid (TCA) peels or phenol peels. The objective is a turnover of the superficial layer and stimulation of collagen growth, without inflammation and other severe skin reactions associated with deep peels.

This is the very same preparation available over the counter under so many trade names. The strength of commercial OTC preparations rarely exceeds 10-percent AHA, which makes them very safe for long-term treatment and maintenance. These are usually maintenance products, such as moisturizers containing AHA. They are not "peels." Estheticians in spas perform peels using up to 30-percent AHA, which results in exfoliation and flaking similar to microdermabrasion. Medical preparations contain up to 70-percent AHA and are quite effective but often caustic and must be carefully controlled. The usual course of treatment for early skin changes, discolorations, and fine wrinkles is a series of office visits at which increasingly strong solutions are used. The alpha hydroxy acid is painted on the skin and left in place for several minutes until a tingling or burning sensation is felt. At that point the solution neutralized, or washed off with cold water, or both. The tingling stops, and the skin may look red for up to a few hours. There is no immediate peeling, though some skin flakes off over the post-peel days. The patient applies a mild AHA preparation nightly to keep up the low-level acid activity, and the cycle is repeated every two-three weeks for six sessions.

The effect of these treatments is cumulative, due to both the increasing strength of the solution used and the repetition of the process. Positive changes are noticed by virtually all patients and the risks are very minimal. An occasional individual may react to the strong solution with a sunburn like effect, but that is fleeting. Transient discoloration has been reported, but that is usually resolved as well; the rare cases of persistent discoloration respond well to treatment with bleaching agents. The overall result is smoother, more lustrous skin free of discoloration, blemishes, surface irregularities, and fine wrinkles.

YOUTH CORRIDOR NO PEEL PEEL

Until recently, the standard AHA peel described above was the treatment I suggested to most patients over thirty years of age. It worked well at cleaning, revitalizing, and rejuvenating the skin and was an important part of an annual "clean up." But recently we began using a unique, and truly game changing addition to the world of AHA peels. The *Youth Corridor No Peel Peel.* This is a 70% glycolic acid solution mixed with another elemental ingredient that renders the solution virtually painless. Full strength peels are tolerated for up to ten minutes without burning or significant tingling. Best of all, the peel has the full effect of a 70-percent glycolic peel with no down time and almost no flaking of dead skin. For most patients our estheticians work up to the full ten minutes, adding peel time with each visit. In rare occasions when the peel is uncomfortable it is quickly neutralized. Patients leave the office actually looking better immediately, and may return to work or the normal activities of the day. As after all peels, they are instructed to use sunscreen, and avoid direct sun exposure for a week. The 70-percent glycolic acid peel is the gold standard as far as getting the job done safely, and the *No Peel Peel* makes it easy. As with all peels, and all treatments, there is the occasional sensitivity reaction, or other minor complication, but they are been few and far between. Anyone who has had glycolic acid peels will immediately become a fan of the *Youth Corridor No Peel Peel.* It's easy, and it's effective, and one doesn't look blotchy and flake for days.

I have found that the best routine for exfoliation is initial dermaplaning and a *No Peel Peel* for the first treatment, followed by peels two weeks apart, for a total of six peels, followed by home maintenance.

As discussed in the section on over-the-counter preparations, you can actually benefit from over-the-counter preparations of AHA as well. They are particularly good for maintaining the status quo after other treatments, and these less-concentrated preparations are a good periodic exfoliant for younger people. They are safe, and the results are visible. Nevertheless, most other over-the-counter preparations are not concentrated enough to be significantly effective, and sometimes they are ineffective.

All the hype you see about each new product changing the nature of the skin, initiating great biochemical changes or renewing collagen are pretty much what they seem, exaggerations just short of being misleading lies. Most work. But they work slowly, and never as well as a professional peel. You must stick with the program. If these preparations entered the substance of the skin in any concentration rather than affecting only the dead cells on the surface, they would be classified as drugs, undergo the scrutiny of the FDA, and they would require a doctor's prescription. An exception to the above is the vitamin C preparations, which are meant to penetrate to the dermis, where they do their work. The problem is getting them to penetrate the epidermis in high enough concentration to be effective. The irony of the position of the alpha hydroxy acids is that they are NOT meant to enter the skin—or, at least, not the deep dermis. They do their exfoliating work on the epidermis, the superficial layer of the skin, and get things going. But they do stimulate collagen production in the superficial dermis.

The limited strength of AHA peels available over-the-counter or at skin-care salons protects the consumer from the dangers of too concentrated an acid peel in unqualified hands, yours or anyone else's.

Since these treatments are not very deep and do not require anesthesia, they are usually performed by the skin-care staff. Fees are fairly modest and currently tend to range between $200 and $300 per session. Six sessions, two-three weeks apart, are recommended for maximum benefit.

DERMAPLANING

This is the most effective exfoliating technique. It is certainly not new, but it does require skill and experience to perform properly. In essence it involves scraping off the layers of dead skin cells with a sterile blade. Not unlike the process of shaving with a straight razor. A frightening picture, but something every man did every morning for centuries. An art lost to the popularity of disposable safety razor. The scraping action physically removes the superficial layer and prepares the skin for more effective peeling.

At the Youth Corridor Clinic our estheticians are practiced in the technique and it is a favored method to get the most from our peels.

TRETINOIN

This is a subject that everyone knows a little bit about, they just don't recognize the name. Tretinoin is the generic name for the active ingredient of Retin-A. The pioneering product was developed at the University of Pennsylvania in the 1960s, and is produced by the Ortho Pharmaceutical Corporation. It has become a part of the beauty jargon. Other products also contain tretinoin, and related compounds have surfaced under various trade names. Therefore, it makes sense to deal with generic names for active ingredients whenever possible.

The product has been around for many years for the treatment of acne. It is an acid derivative of vitamin A and has properties that cause the skin cells to turn over in a manner that suggests youthful behavior. With regular use the outer, visible, keratinized layer becomes smoother, less irregular and thinner. Some blemishes disappear, and, over the course of several weeks, fine wrinkles, and areas of rough skin diminish. Tretinoin may also increase the ability of the skin to produce and lay down collagen within the dermis.

Tretinoin therapy is usually begun with 0.025-percent cream. It is applied nightly to dry skin twenty minutes after proper cleansing. It is applied thinly in an invisible layer. The original preparation was exceedingly drying; Renova, another formulation of the drug (and it is a drug), is less irritating. This would be advantageous to those unable to tolerate the irritation caused by the original formulation. For effects to be visible, the treatment must continue for at least six weeks, though longer-term use is the rule. Often, increasingly higher-strength creams are used until the level of tolerance is reached. During and for a period of time after treatment, the skin is increasingly sensitive to sun exposure and must be protected by sunscreen. If that is not scrupulously adhered to, blotchy pigmentation may result.

It is not entirely understood whether the use of tretinoin needs to become a permanent part of a long-term routine to achieve and maintain maximal results. It seems wise to allow the skin time to recover from the treatment. Others advise that the effectiveness is based on forcing the skin into more youthful behavior patterns and therefore should be continual. There is significant overlap in the effect of tretinoin and the alpha hydroxy acids upon wrinkles, skin pigmentation, and blemishes, irregularities of the skin surface, and the quality and quantity of the collagen and elastin within the dermis. Tretinoin, or other retinoids, are frequently used for several weeks before TCA peels as peeled skin pretreated with tretinoin heals faster and shows greater improvement.

Tretinoin is perhaps the least invasive of the physician-regulated therapies. It actually straddles a fine line, since it is prescription-controlled but patient-applied and self-evaluated and regulated. Less-potent vitamin A derivatives, called retinoids, can be found in many skin-care lines. It is still necessary to purchase tretinoin products from pharmacies with doctors' prescriptions or directly from physicians. Your dermatologist or plastic surgeon should play some role in monitoring your progress, and periodic visits after the initial three months are in order; also, the strength of the cream or its frequency of application may be altered. Once these variables are determined, long-term therapy is usually well tolerated.

Other tretinoin retinoid products include Avita and Atralin, which are marketed primarily as acne treatments, the use for which tretinoin was originally developed. Both prescription tretinoin and over the counter retinoid products are effective against acne because of their ability to reduce the heaping up of keratinocytes (dead skin cells) at the surface of oil glands, reduce inflammation, and thereby prevent, or reverse acne.

There is a natural ability of the body to convert all retinoid products to the active, natural, tretinoin form. The primary difference is the strength, and hence the effectiveness of the product. *Retinultimate*, the Youth Corridor retinoid gel, has proven extremely effective as an acne fighting agent. Currently, it has been adapted for effectively treating fine lines, skin irregularities, and blemishes. The remarkable aspect of this elegant gel is the ability to function very effectively without irritation. *Youth Corridor Retinultimate* gel feels wonderful on the skin, works well in concert with our AHA products, and augments the effects of vitamin C serum. Is *Retinultimate* as strong as Retin A (tretinoin)? No, it is not. But it is far less irritating, easier to use, and a perfect part of a good skin care routine.

Bleaching Creams, Lightening Agents, and Brighteners

Melanin is the substance responsible for pigment in the skin. Obviously, shades of skin color vary between ethnic groups, and individuals, and are genetically determined. Irregular areas of pigmentation break the continuum of any color, and catch the eye. For fair-skinned individuals, these dark areas contrast sharply with the basic coloration. The pigmented areas may take any of a number of forms, most of which are unattractive but are mostly of no true medical significance. For many of these problems, there are reasonably effective methods to control excess pigmentation.

On the other hand, little progress has been made in the treatment of pigment-depletion problems. This often spontaneous pigment loss is called vitiligo. Loss of pigment is particularly noticeable, and disturbing to dark-skinned individuals. Pigment loss is not always genetic. It can also result from peels, laser resurfacing or other medical treatments.

Hyperpigmentation, the accumulation of excess pigment, has many known causes. These include sun exposure, response to hormone mimicking medications such as birth control pills, natural hormone changes, and even surgery. A typical problem is the forehead and cheek pigmentation called melasma. It is often related to pregnancy or birth control pills and is known as "the mask of pregnancy," but photo damage...sunlight...plays a significant role in this distressing, and very common problem.

The most effective treatment for pigmentation is the use of bleaching creams. Bleaching creams work by inhibiting the enzyme tyrosinase, which is necessary for the production of melanin and hence pigment. The most frequently used products are based on the compound hydroquinone, which interferes with pigment production. Application of hydroquinone to dark spots causes the melanocytes in the skin to reduce melanin production. This process takes at least four weeks to show results, since the old pigmented cells must be shed before the new, lighter cells surface. So bleaching agent is a misnomer. Nothing is bleached; the new crop of skin cells is less pigmented, and the dark areas recede.

Hydroquinone is prescription-regulated in its effective 4-percent strength. It is used primarily as a spot treatment, applied to the hyperpigmented area only, and not the entire face, and its use should be discussed with a physician. While using hydroquinone therapy, sun exposure must be avoided. That can be done by actually avoiding sunlight or with sunblock. Sunlight would be self-defeating as it promotes pigmentation. Some manufacturers deal with this by adding sunscreen to the hydroquinone preparation, which seems like a very sensible solution.

Another, very effective bleaching agent is niacinamide, a form of vitamin B3. Studies have shown it to be nearly as effective as hydroquinone. Niacinamide also works by interfering with the production of melanin as well as with the biology of melanocytes. It is effective as an anti-wrinkle and anti-photodamage ingredient as well. As a side bar, recent studies have shown oral niacinamide to markedly reduce the incidence of skin cancers in people prone to developing basal cell carcinomas. It also bolsters the basal lipid barrier, which helps retain moisture, and builds collagen to fight wrinkles. There seems to be nothing but good things to say about the use of niacinamide in skin care, and it has become part of the formulation of *Youth Corridor Ultimate Antioxidant C Boost*. This makes a lot of sense both for the properties of niacinamide alone, and the fact that it is increasingly effective when combined with vitamin C.

Irregular areas of skin pigmentation are far more common a problem than one would imagine. It is more prevalent in women due the hormonal effect of birth control pills and pregnancy. Drug reactions and sun exposure account for much of the incidence as well. Some individuals have naturally occurring dark under-eye circles, while others have sun-related age spots. In all but the most glaring situations, women tend to cover the areas with makeup, and men tend to ignore them altogether. The availability of simple, effective treatment has begun to offer hope. In most situations, superficial peels help relieve the problem, but the first line of defense should be lightening creams and serums, and sunblock. Currently, hydroquinone is the strongest, most reliable bleaching agent available. Unfortunately, it is not without side effects beyond its irritant qualities. There have been reports of possible carcinogenic activity in animals, related to hydroquinone, and though not adequately documented in humans, hydroquinone use has been controlled. Hydroquinone is still available in up to 2-percent concentration over the counter, which calls into question how seriously the FDA considers the risk. It has been banned in Europe.

Safe bleaching agents made of naturally occurring botanicals have become popular and are available in many skin-care lines. The pigment-bleaching action is not as strong as hydroquinone, but the ingredients tend to "brighten" the overall look of the skin, and the effect is positive. The botanical agents, which gradually even out skin tone, are applied to the entire surface of the face, not just the darker areas, and result in a generally lighter and more even pigment. They work by inhibiting tyrosine metabolism, which is similar to the action of hydroquinone. This is a long-term undertaking, so expect to wait six to eight weeks before a significant change is noted in dark areas. A generalized "brightening" of the skin is visible much sooner. Glutathione, a powerful antioxidant has shown great potential as a lightening agent; however, it is difficult to deliver the active form through the skin. Using glutathione in combination with vitamin C seems to improve efficacy, but a stable and effective combination remains elusive. Kojic acid is a good lightening agent, but it is extremely unstable when exposed to air, and rapidly loses its effectiveness. Most products containing kojic acid use a more stable, but virtually ineffective form. Other lightening and brightening agents include numerous botanical extracts, including whatever seems to be the berry of the moment. All of these ingredients work a little. None work particularly well in available concentrations.

The best of the lightening-brightening agents...hydroquinone aside...are vitamin C, niacinamide, and glycolic acid. These products are an integral part of the Youth Corridor program, and they are incorporated in our products where ever possible.

HUMAN GROWTH HORMONE

Human growth hormone as an anti-aging strategy is the stuff of science fiction. Hundreds of thousands of older adults have gotten on the bandwagon, persuaded by seemingly reasonable advertisements that the fountain of youth was an injection away, and many more have been persuaded to believe that it was only a pill from their grasp. Unfortunately, it seems that although the facts are pure science, the therapeutic results, alas, may be fiction, or at least wishful thinking. Since the seeds of possibility do exist, small cults of believers have arisen. The use of growth hormone for rejuvenation has burst the confines of scientific conjecture and landed on the front page of *The Wall Street Journal*. Claims of miraculous rejuvenation of every sort have been made. People are using it, and other people are making large sums of money providing it, so we should start at the beginning and try to understand the facts.

Human growth hormone is produced by the acidophilic cells of the anterior portion of the pituitary gland within the brain. This master gland, as it is called, functions by producing and circulating hormones that stimulate endocrine glands to produce other hormones that directly affect bodily functions. Its signals set the adrenal and thyroid glands to work and generally act to regulate hormone activity. One of the substances produced is growth hormone, which triggers activity in the growth centers of the bones and in secondary supporting structures, such as muscles. Not very long ago, it was found that children and young adults with stunted growth could be pushed toward normal growth by the injection of growth hormone. The success of the therapy was based on correcting the relatively low level of the hormone produced naturally. It was a big step forward, and specifically aimed at treatment of growth defects. It was also known that in normally developed individuals, growth hormone production drops off rapidly after adolescence; however, a continual level can be expected throughout adulthood. Some adults have lower levels of growth hormone than others, which sowed the seed for an interesting study. A small number of men in their fifties and sixties with reduced levels of circulating growth hormone were treated with injections of the substance and their progress monitored. The results varied from interesting to surprising.

The subjects reported a general sense of well-being and mood elevation. Interesting, but not a big deal. Lots of substances of real and imagined potency can do that. But increased bone density and a measurable increase in muscle mass also occurred. Instead of wasting with age, these men were growing, bulking up, showing increased sexual activity and, in short, responding to growth hormone in an age-defying manner, particularly regarding libido and skin texture. Exciting? You bet. But don't start getting injections yet. There is more to the story.

Unfortunately, the studies done to date have been very small, and very inconclusive. A 2005 study in *JAMA* examined more recent data and stated that the increases in lean muscle mass and decrease in body fat "were transient and modest and in one study disappeared after 24 months." There was also a measurable increase in skin elasticity, interesting as well. All studies identify numerous side effects. Among them were breast development in males, carpal tunnel syndrome (a painful and debilitating entrapment of the median nerve at the wrist), muscle and joint pain, glucose intolerance, and elevated triglycerides in the blood.

"So what?" you say. "I'll gladly deal with those problems and stay young forever."

Not so fast. Another reported side effect from the growth hormone treatment, though rare, is grotesque overgrowth of the face. The bones actually enlarge, and the features expand. That is not such good news. Prudent investigators put it all together and advised the need for time for reevaluation. Charlatans and dreamers moved full steam ahead. In fact, a number of well-trained and thoughtful practitioners have begun offering this therapy to their patients, but they are a distinct minority. Growth hormone sales have been estimated at $2 billion yearly—most of it in the form of pills and sprays, which have been clearly shown to be unable to deliver HGH into the bloodstream. The only effective method of delivery is by injection, which is the way HGH is provided for children with a proven deficiency. Pills, capsules and sprays are a waste of time and money. Injectable HGH remains fascinating, and I am convinced that you will be hearing more and more about this exciting and dangerous dream in the very near future. My advice? Wait and see. Too many people have been stimulated by the possibilities for it to go unexplored, but don't take a risk that could be devastating to your health. There are so many physician believers providing HGH for this off-label use that more information is bound to surface.

NINE

Trouble Spots

The preceding chapters have laid the groundwork for what is available for skin care and self-help. In our artificial segmentation into Prevention, Maintenance, and Correction, we are now entering the realm of maintenance and correction. Here we will identify the trouble spots, hopefully as they first make themselves known, and deal with them before they cause indelible changes. This is newer thinking. It is aimed at *minimal intervention* and *maintenance*. If you begin early and follow this schedule through the years, you may never need more than minor procedures to keep looking your best. If you begin at forty or later, when changes have been allowed to occur, it may ultimately lead to a limited-incision face-lift. This is something you may accept or reject, but if you follow the program to that point of decision you will surely look far better along the way than had you not followed the program at all.

This fact applies to any stage. You will always benefit from the effort and interest you have invested. Despite the fact that aging ultimately rears its unwelcome head, you will always look better than your "identical twin," who didn't follow the program. Some of the techniques we will explore are relatively new; most have been around for a while. All have often been considered as ancillary procedures to be performed when surgery is considered later in life. In my practice, I have found it useful to isolate these treatments and apply them individually as trouble spots surface. I find that these small procedures are most useful for keeping younger people looking young. Save your mini face-lift for your sixtieth birthday.

Here is the list of annoying changes we can all expect. They will be manifested at different times for different individuals, but few are immune. Don't worry, you won't have them all, and they won't all happen at once. I have tried to follow the chronological order of appearance, keeping the worst for last. Don't sneak a look at the mirror and get depressed. Here's where the trouble starts.

1. Smile lines, or squint lines outside eyes.
2. Vertical lines between the eyebrows (glabellar frown lines).
3. Blotchy, lack-luster skin.
4. Fine wrinkles under eyes
5. Discoloration or abnormal pigmentation.
6. Deepening nasolabial lines or folds from corners of nostrils to corners of mouth.
7. Parenthesis-like lines at corners of mouth, and marionette lines from the mouth corners toward the jawline.
8. Vertical lines in upper lip.
9. Fullness or jowls along the jawline, causing loss of clean, straight look.
10. Fullness under jaw, looseness of skin, or double chin.
11. Small fatty pouches alongside mouth

Any one of these signs alone is unpleasant, but not the end of the world. Untreated, these early signs of aging deepen, loosen, and generally get worse until the happy face of youth is lost. How discouraging. I have magnified and compressed the changes, but this is reality. The following chapters will help you understand why this doesn't have to happen and how we intend to stop all these changes before they take hold.

This drawing illustrates many changes listed here.

TEN

Maintenance

The section on prevention was primarily concerned with lifestyle changes, good skin care, at home peels, and the like. In the maintenance section, we will be dealing with professional office treatments: injectables, peels, lasers, and minimally invasive procedures. These are professionally performed, office-based measures.

INJECTABLES

Botox has been all the rage since it was approved by the FDA in 2002, and for good reason, it works. It is simply the most effective temporary method to smooth out frown lines and wrinkles caused by the action of the muscles of facial expression. Frighteningly enough, this safe substance is produced from botulism toxin, a deadly poison. Though no longer toxic, the substance retains the ability to temporarily paralyze the nerves and muscles it supplies. It can be injected into the corrugator muscles, which cause frown lines between the eyebrows; the frontalis muscle, which wrinkles the forehead; and the orbicularis oculi muscle, which creates smile lines; and for a period of time it irons out the wrinkles by acting on the nerve supply and paralyzing the muscles that cause wrinkles by their contraction. A successful treatment usually lasts between four and six months, and the results, which are seen within 48 hours, are quite dramatic. Sometimes, too dramatic. There are altogether too many people who have been "over Botoxed" and are totally wrinkle-free, motion free—and look frighteningly unnatural.

Botox is so effective that common sense and experience are crucial when using it. For all users, including the most knowledgeable and best intentioned, there is always the risk of an imbalance of one side compared with the other or early recovery of one side. This makes for a distorted and unpleasant outcome, requiring additional injections to restore balance. Another problem frequently seen is drooping eyebrows after Botox injections. This is caused by injecting either too much, or too close to the eyebrows. Sometimes it is better to leave the lowest forehead wrinkle as it is rather than take this risk. To correct this effect it is possible to raise the eyebrow by injecting beneath it and releasing the muscle that pulls the eyebrow down.

As often as I have performed this maneuver, there are still occasions when some level of imbalance persists. The good news is that the effect begins to wear off in eight to twelve weeks or can be dealt with by injecting competing muscles. As the physician becomes more experienced, complications occur less frequently.

My staff of trained nurse injectors and I employ Botox primarily to treat horizontal forehead lines, the vertical furrows between the eyebrows, and smile or squint lines outside the eyes. Sometimes I use a drop of Botox to treat the excessive dimpling of the skin on the chin that some people develop, or to lessen lip wrinkling, and I have found it useful to soften the vertical platysma bands of the neck. Botox is also useful to control excessive underarm perspiration, which it does by paralyzing the tiny muscles in the sweat glands.

For many young people with familial tendencies to wrinkling caused by facial muscle use…rather than the fine wrinkling of sun exposure and age…Botox is a preventative strategy. People as young as their early twenties sometimes show signs of smile lines and frown lines. If untreated, these will shortly become deep, permanent facial lines. The use of small amounts of Botox in these areas can stop the wrinkles before they form. **The best way to treat a wrinkle is to prevent it,** and here is a circumstance where we can do just that.

Botox is an FDA-approved wrinkle treatment. Reconstituted from powder only as directed and injected at full strength, the full effect is seen in forty-eight hours, and begins to wane after three-four months. In five or six months, the effects are usually gone completely. After a few sessions doctor and patient develop a routine and are able to get the desired result with the fewest treatments. Some people restrict patient's activities after treatment. I do not believe this is necessary. There are very rare, very sensational reports of serious complications associated with Botox use. To my knowledge most are unproven, circumstantial, and do not seem to represent a significant drawback to its use. Millions of injections have proven it safe and successful.

There are neurotoxins other than Botox that do essentially the same thing, the same way. These products include Dysport, and Zeomin, with others waiting in the wings. I have no experience with the other products, simply because they offer nothing significantly new, and are no more attractively priced than Botox, which is expensive for physician and patient. If something better comes along you will know about it. This is a multi-billion dollar market, and all the big players want a part of it. So far, nothing has any advantage over Botox.

It's difficult to estimate the average price of Botox treatments, since this depends on the extent of the areas to be treated, the concentration used, and the doctor. Treating glabellar frown lines alone could cost as little as $250-350 per session, while treating full forehead, frown lines and smile lines could cost as much as $2000. The substance itself is quite expensive, and much of the price difference between doctors is a function of how much they dilute the basic Botox concentrate. Botox is supplied in a dried form, and 100 units is meant to be diluted with 2ccs of sterile saline to be full strength. If you are shopping around, ask about the dilution used. Know that 50 units per cc is full strength.

Sometimes people think they are getting a bargain, when they are actually getting an over diluted product.

FILLERS

After peels, fillers and Botox are usually the first professional anti-aging service that most people seek when they are trying to address early wrinkles and developing folds. The use of fillers to combat nasolabial folds and frown lines has been enormously popular since the introduction of injectable collagen in 1975. Fillers are useful in treating marionette lines, those nasty lines and folds running down from the corners of the mouth, and fillers are fashionable for plumping up lips and softening lip lines.

Here is how fillers work: Beneath the epidermis—the outer, protective layer of skin—is the dermis. This fairly thick layer contains blood vessels, and lubricating and sweat glands within a matrix of collagen fibers. Collagen comprises the bulk of the substance of the skin, and keeps it plump, wrinkle free, and healthy looking. The breakdown of collagen causes, sagging, wrinkling, loss of elasticity, and furrows, so it would seem worthwhile to try to replace the loss. Numerous substances and techniques have been developed in the attempt to smooth wrinkles, fill furrows, and replace lost or denatured collagen. All are good, and none are perfect—the only filler with any level of permanence is your own tissue, in the form of a fat transfer. But more about that later.

The following group of fillers encompasses most of the popular injectables. They share the convenience of a "quick fix," rarely requiring more than a few minutes in the doctor's office, a series of fine pinpricks and little to no downtime. Despite my enthusiasm for the immediate improvement afforded, I always remind my patients that the filler will dissipate in three to six months.

Cosmoplast and Cosmoderm. The search for the perfect replacement material has been going on for decades, since the introduction of injectable collagen derived from bovine skin. Despite the fact that the actual proteins comprising cow collagen are similar to ours and are very well tolerated, there was a slight, but worrisome, incidence of allergy. The need for subcutaneous skin injection in the forearm to detect allergy, a waiting and observation period, and the fleeting stability of the injected collagen made the product less than ideal. But it was all that we had.

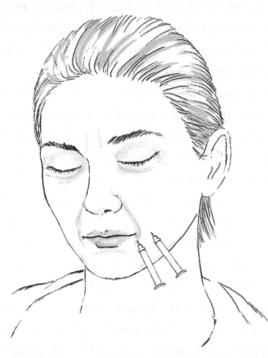

Fillers are effective treatment for nasolabial folds and lip and vertical frown lines.

The original collagen morphed into a longer lasting product called Zyplast, which eventually was superseded by Cosmoderm and Cosmoplast, both derived from purified human collagen and essentially allergy-free. Both products contain a little lidocaine, which dulls the pain of injection, but since they are injected into the dermis, as are all these products, the pain is not much more than a pin stick. As with all the products in this section, a topical anesthetic can be applied to the skin fifteen minutes before injection; most people do not need it. Cosmoplast and Cosmoderm differ slightly in thickness. Cosmoderm is suggested for more superficial wrinkles. Both products last three to six months. (Think four to five months, and you won't be disappointed.) The cost of a 1cc syringe, which is enough to treat both nasolabial folds, is between $450 and $1000.

With the advent of hyaluronic acid fillers, I have abandoned collagen based products. Why? Because they seem to last longer, and don't have the history of allergy to explain. **Restylane, the first in the category,** challenged and unseated the collagen products as the most popular filler from the moment it was introduced. The initial welcome was because it was not associated with allergy. It was the first of the hyaluronic acid products and remains a leader in the field, if not the leader. Hyaluronic acid is a naturally occurring space-occupying substance found in the skin and joints. As such, it should be ideal as a filler to replace lost volume—except that it is expensive, and it too disappears in a matter of months.

Restylane is produced by bacteria. Other hyaluronic acid products are of animal or bacterial origin; all are FDA approved, and all are safe. Initially, Restylane was thought to be much longer lasting than the collagen products, and that added to its appeal. In actual practice, Restylane lasts up to six months. It is good for the treatments of folds and wrinkles at the dermal level. Restylane can be used to plump and fill large areas, as can all the other fillers, but the cost associated and the lack of permanent result make it less than optimal for this particular use. The cost of a 1cc Restylane treatment is between $450 and $1000. Perlane, from the same manufacturer, is thicker than Restylane and is suggested for deeper folds; it is available at the same cost.

Juvéderm is another hyaluronic acid product. It is not unlike Restylane, but is a smooth, denser gel. It is meant to be injected into the dermis of the skin to fill and soften deep wrinkles and furrows. The skin may be anesthetized slightly with a topical cream before injection, but since the injections are fairly deep they are not as uncomfortable as those placed in fine, superficial wrinkles. Juvéderm is supplied in 1cc syringes. Typically, two syringes are necessary to fill out nasolabial lines, glabellar lines, "parentheses" at the corners of the mouth and marionette lines. Juvéderm is also used to plump lips and fill defects.

It may last a bit longer than Restylane but rarely much more than six months. Juvéderm treatment costs between $500 and $1000 per syringe.

Another excellent application of hyaluronic acid filler is to fill the tear trough, the deep circles under the eyes that give one a tired appearance. This is a delicate matter, and should only be done by experienced professionals.

Hyaluronic acid fillers are also used to enlarge lips, accentuate the "white line" of the lips, and fill in vertical lip lines. Vertical lip lines are difficult to fully correct this way. Numerous injections, with a very fine needle, are necessary to place exactly the correct amount of filler into very fine lines. Since the lips are so sensitive a numbing cream is applied for all but the most stoic patients.

All the above fillers are temporary. That's bad and good. Bad, because they must be replenished every few months, and good, because if the result is less than perfect, it dissipates and you don't have to live with it forever. Misplaced, or excessive hyaluronic acid filler can be easily reversed with the direct injection of an enzyme that dissolves the substance, but this is rarely necessary.

Voluma is a Juvéderm relative. It's a bit thicker and possibly longer lasting. It is meant to augment deeper tissues. Typically it can be used in the nasolabial folds or to build up cheekbones. I have found Voluma to be the best of the "store bought" volume replacers. Three or four ccs of Voluma and cheekbone angularity is significantly augmented, creating a youthful, angular look. The substance is by no means a permanent solution, but the immediate result can be great. I have also found it useful for building up the chin a bit. Voluma costs from $1250-$2500 per cc.

Radiesse is different from other fillers in that it is specific for correcting deep defects. Composed of calcium microspheres called hydroxyapatite, which is related to bone substance, it is injected with a larger-bore needle and local anesthetic is used in the areas of injection. This adds very little time to the treatment and is no more uncomfortable than the other fillers. The product is suggested for nasolabial lines and dermal filling. In my experience, it serves best in areas where deep buildup is needed—never superficially. Radiesse lasts more than a year and costs $1000-$1500 per syringe.

Sculptra is derived from lactic acid, one of the alpha hydroxy acids. It was originally marketed to treat the dermal fat wasting associated with HIV infection. Sculptra is used in fairly large volumes, fills the void where normal skin substance has dissipated, and encourages collagen production, and it lasts up to two years, sometimes more. Obviously, this was seen as good news, and the product was adopted by many as an off-label cosmetic filler. It lived up to its claims for longevity, but as it was used in multiple doses, it stimulated collagen growth, and lumps in the skin were sometimes felt and occasionally seen. Some of these have been very long-lasting, and troublesome. Sculptra has been primarily used to replace deep-tissue loss but has recently been approved by the FDA for facial folds and wrinkles. I do not believe it is interchangeable with Restylane, Juvéderm, and the others, and I have not used it for these purposes.

A NOTE OF CAUTION ABOUT FILLERS: Fillers are surely a quick fix. They can do wonders when appropriately used. The problem is that fillers, like Botox, can be overused and abused. While there is no inherent danger of physical harm, the fine line between filling-in folds or augmenting cheek bones can be easily crossed, making things look worse, not better. Altogether too frequently we see people with what some jokingly refer to as "filler face." Absurdly large cheekbones or unnaturally pouty lips are exaggerated features that make for an eye-catching, but unsightly appearance. Yes, adding volume to cheekbones gives angularity, and a lift, but carrying anything to absurd limits makes no sense at all. This is all about looking your best, not looking silly. Overdone fillers dissipate in months, or can be dissolved with enzyme injection. That's the nature of the product. The good news and the bad news is that fillers only last months.

FAT TRANSFER

Fat Transfer, autologous fat transfer, in medical jargon, refers to the process of transferring living fat cells from a donor area to another area that needs filling, or volume augmentation, on the same person. Some thirty-five percent of the transferred fat remains in place as a PERMANENT, natural filler. And fifty to seventy-five percent is permanent when injected into areas with particularly rich blood supply. Since it is your fat, there is no danger of allergy. Large quantities can be used when necessary, and the results are natural. I firmly believe in fat transfer, it is the best of all available fillers, but the process is not as simple as the five minutes necessary for injection of commercial fillers.

The concept behind fat transfer is that the live, transferred, fat cells will find a blood supply in the new area and live there permanently, filling in wrinkles and folds and plumping out the skin. The process must be carried out carefully, under sterile conditions. Numerous injections of local anesthetic are required, and most patients require sedation to make the procedure more pleasant. It doesn't take very long, causes very little swelling, no pain, and no significant downtime, and results are generally excellent. I believe it is far and away the best of the fillers and is a major part of the Youth Corridor antiaging strategy.

With aging, we all lose and redistribute fat padding and facial volume. This results in a decrease in angularity and a slackness, symptomatic of the older face. Fat is the perfect solution to replace exactly what has been lost. It is also the longest lasting filler for deep nasolabial and glabellar frown lines. Autologous fat is invaluable for volume restoration and augmenting cheekbones and chin. Used this way, fat transfer can lift and rejuvenate the face as it enhances features and fills in defects.

In the procedure, a small amount of fat, usually 10-20 ccs, is removed by syringe from one body area, usually where you have more than enough to spare…usually hips or belly… and transplanted by injection to an area that needs to be filled in, usually facial wrinkles, lip lines, lips, folds or frown lines, cheekbones or chin. Before your imagination runs away with you, here are the ground rules. To begin with, the fat must be transferred from one place to another on the same individual. That means that you can't lend to, or borrow from, your friends. There is also the issue of blood supply. The only transplanted fat that survives is that portion that develops a blood supply in its new location, and that requires being in nearly direct contact with the tiny blood vessels of the area. The more distant a portion of transplanted fat is from the existing capillaries, the less likely it is to survive. Millimeters make a difference. To this end, tiny amounts are transplanted at different levels making use of proximity to blood supply. The strategy works. I have performed well in excess of ten thousand fat transfers, and find my patients consistently delighted with the results.

Yes, you can take excess fat from your thighs and enlarge your breasts. It takes innumerable injections, but it is being done increasingly frequently, and with great success. The primary problem with this procedure had been the calcifications that develop within the transplanted fat and breast tissue. Initially, it had been difficult to differentiate these calcifications from calcifications indicative of breast cancer. But recent advances in imaging techniques, and experience, have increased the level of confidence radiologists have in differentiating the types of calcification, and it is no longer an issue.

Large volumes of fat are harvested from abdomen, buttocks, or hips…in this case enough to make a positive change…and are serially injected into the breast under anesthesia. There are protocols which stretch breast skin to allow the accommodation of the new volume, and usually more than one session is necessary. Interestingly, there appears to be a critical volume, beyond which fat "take" falls off. This speaks to the need for the transplanted fat to be close enough to blood vessels to find nourishment, in order to survive. Autologous fat breast augmentation is being done with increasing frequency and has become part of the plastic surgeon's tool kit.

As noted above, for a transplanted fat cell to survive, it must receive a blood supply from the tissue against which it rests. The farther from that living tissue and blood vessels or the thicker the transplant, the less likely is success. Here we are not talking about inches, but fractions of fractions of an inch. Skin grafts survive free transfer about 0.5 millimeters from the blood supply. Twenty-five millimeters equal about one inch, so we are talking about one fiftieth of an inch. One can assume fat transplants of at least twice that thickness survive, since theoretically there is blood supply from both above and below. So we arrive at one twenty-fifth of an inch or a bit more. In actual practice, most fat transplants are far thicker than that. That is so for many reasons. First, the caliber of the needle used is fairly large so as not to crush the cells. Then the delivery mechanism is not very precise.

Here is a practical example: A patient wants the deep nasolabial line from the corner of the nose to the mouth filled in. So we fill it in. What happens? Well, as you might expect, the line or fold virtually disappears. It looks great for six months, but then some of the line begins to reappear as the fat that hasn't established a blood supply gets absorbed. Beyond the layer that survives, the rest of the fat has served as temporary filler, but in most cases we estimate that up to 35 percent of the fat will survive permanently. Fat injections, done twice over a period of eighteen months, usually offer a very good permanent correction of the defect. Most of the correction is due to a take of the transplanted fat and a bit to a fibrous tissue that builds up at the site of injection. In my experience, most people need to repeat the procedure at least twice, sometimes more. Areas with active movement, like the nasolabial folds, may require repeated treatment. After a fat transfer, we wait six months to see how much has been a permanent take. As a rule, whatever remains at that time will be permanent.

Fat transfer is a simple office procedure. It can be performed under local anesthesia, but more usually with a little intravenous sedation for comfort. I usually suggest sedation. A fat-donor site is chosen—usually the thigh, buttock, or abdomen. The area is injected with local anesthetic, a special needle is inserted and a small amount of fat is removed by gentle manual suction. Not enough fat is removed to create a defect, and care is taken to preserve symmetry. The fat is centrifuged to separate oils from fat cells. The oil is discarded and multiple small syringes are filled with the fat. The site for treatment is prepared and anesthetized, and the fat is injected in numerous tiny droplets. The entire procedure takes about half an hour. There is little swelling or discoloration and one can plan on returning to work the next day. It is usually a good idea to very slightly overcorrect the area to compensate for swelling and the local anesthetic. Significant overcorrection can make the result last somewhat longer, but it looks unnatural, and I do not choose that option for my patients. <u>The rule in cosmetic surgery should be: If it doesn't look natural, it isn't worth doing.</u>

Then there is the question of harvesting large amounts of fat, freezing it, and administering it over time. That makes very little sense, as there is no evidence that the fat cells survive freezing; therefore the injections are merely filler. Physicians employing frozen fat inject it weekly or monthly and claim a connective-tissue buildup at the site, which may be marginally accurate. Thus far, there is no objective evidence to support this contention; still, at worst one is being treated with a very transient natural filler.

The critical question is which lasts longer: fat, Juvéderm, Cosmoplast, Restylane, or the others? Fat lasts longer. A significant percentage of injected fat resides permanently in the injection site. Both commercial fillers and injected fat give visible improvement for up to six months; but while the fat persists, the other fillers disappear. A percentage of the transplanted fat dissipates by this time, but some of it lasts forever. That is the key, and it is something on which to build for a permanent correction.

Over the long run, fat transfers are far superior. If you stick with it and have the procedure repeated, you will get a significant degree of permanent correction. The cost of fat transplants varies widely but averages between $5000 and $10000 per session. Considering the permanence of the result and the larger volume that is injected, fat transfer is the ultimately the most economical choice of filler, despite its much higher initial cost. At our clinic, the policy is to inject as many areas as necessary for the same fee, as set up and harvesting represent the most time and labor intensive aspect of the procedure. That often means augmenting cheekbones and chin at the same time as filling in lines and folds, and the fees begin to fall in line with multiple-syringe filler use. Many physicians subscribe to this philosophy, and many include fat transfers as part of any facial rejuvenation surgery.

OTHER OFFICE PROCEDURES

Tear Trough Correction

The tear trough is the semicircular hollow under the eyes. When one has puffy lower lids above the trough it is accentuated, and creates a tired or dissipated look. There are any number of ways of correcting this during surgery, but it can also be efficiently dealt with during an office visit with the use of fillers. For these reasons the topic will be referenced again in the surgery section. Filling the trough with one of the hyaluronic acid requires minimal topical anesthetic and tiny droplets of filler delivered through a very fine needle. The procedure takes less than half an hour to perform, and the result can last for up to eighteen months. Permanent correction can be achieved by filling with fat. Some patients elect correction with hyaluronic acid filler first, and if the result is as expected, follow six months later with permanent correction with fat.

Another minor maintenance procedure is microdermabrasion. It is performed by a skin-care specialist and is a popular, noninvasive procedure administered in most aesthetic centers. It is different from a chemical peel in method and depth. In this process a fine powdered substance is applied across the skin under mild pressure, resulting in the physical removal of debris and dead cells on the surface of the skin. This is not a true peel but a skin treatment that patients love, and it offers excellent, if limited, results in reducing superficial skin irregularities. Repeated treatments are excellent in lessening skin blemishes and discolorations, and one is able to face society immediately after treatments. Occasionally, some areas are mildly irritated, but this rapidly dissipates. We feel that six treatments, spaced at least two weeks apart, are optimal. The series is repeated every year or so. Combined with regular low-concentration AHA peels, the improvement in clarity and appearance of one's skin is dramatic, but one peel or one microdermabrasion is not enough. Like everything else, this is a process. One trip to the gym won't improve your muscle tone the same way an exercise routine does. Think about skin treatments the same way.

Aestheticians and spas across the country are offering microdermabrasion and swear by it. The procedure reduces surface irregularities and dead cells, but don't expect it to miraculously remove wrinkles or tighten sagging skin. Treatment costs vary from $150 to $250.

The reality is that microdermabrasion has been phased out of most skin treatment centers. In the Youth Corridor Clinic the microdermabrasion machine has been relegated to the storage closet. Instead, we achieve far better results with the *No Peel Peel* and the newest IPL and laser technology.

DEEP SKIN PEELS

Deep skin peels include a range of options. I tend to use the term to differentiate the category from superficial peels, such alpha hydroxy acid peels, and the *No Peel Peel*, discussed earlier. Deep peels are obviously more aggressive and are designed to work more deeply into the skin in an effort to eliminate wrinkles and equalize skin pigment. But before you jump to the conclusion that deeper is better, you need to know something about the reality of peels.

The concept of deep skin peeling is an attempt to remove the damaged and denatured cells and collagen of the epidermis and superficial dermis and replace them with a smoother and healthier version. This actually works. It not only eliminates wrinkles, but produces tighter, more elastic, and evenly pigmented skin. In the early years of cosmetic surgery and dermatology, the primary peeling agent in widespread use was a phenol-based solution. This is a very caustic agent that essentially dissolves the epidermis and superficial dermis, taking along with the cellular debris both superficial and deep wrinkles. The actual mechanism of healing produces good, thick, well-aligned bands of elastic collagen in the dermis that are far stronger and healthier than the collagen present before peeling. In this manner the skin becomes rejuvenated, better looking, and more resilient.

Being quite effective, the phenol peel should be a most useful tool. Unfortunately, the depth of peel was difficult to control and associated with a whole list of complications. Some of these complications, like loss of pigment and irregular peel depth, are not uncommon. If this isn't enough to make one reject phenol peels, the worst of the complications is phenol-induced cardiac arrhythmia. For most of us, phenol peels are history, and there is rarely any reason to consider them. Recently, dilute phenol peels, in combination with other agents, are being sold in kit form for aesthetician use. With so many safer options, the whole idea of phenol peels leaves me cold.

One of the most effective substitutes for phenol is trichloroacetic acid, or TCA. TCA peels are easier to manage and are considerably safer than phenol peels, but they are not risk-free. The major upside is that the TCA peels produce less color loss than phenol, and the concentration can be varied for application to different problem areas of the face. That is important since skin thickness varies considerably in different locations. The areas around the eyes and eyelids have very fine, thin skin; therefore, one can safely use weaker concentrations of TCA to revitalize those areas. Usually concentrations of 25-percent to 35-percent are employed.

Patients are often routinely pretreated with Retin-A, or other retinoids, and vitamin C serum prior to TCA peels. This seems to enhance efficacy and promote rapid healing. As with all deep peels, the procedure is performed under well-monitored conditions, usually with the patient sedated. These are not procedures for home or the beauty salon.

As far as the patient is concerned, there is a significant upside to the TCA peel. First of all, the post-peel period is significantly less hideous than phenol peels and quite effective. True, the skin swells, but not nearly as much. A brownish layer of dead skin develops, which is covered by ointment or Vaseline, and separates with washing. New skin appears in less than a week, and makeup can then be used to cover the pink cast that persists for several weeks. All in all, it is a quicker and less traumatic experience. On balance, TCA seems to be the peel of choice for aggressively treating facial wrinkles and blemishes, though some physicians have switched to concentrated AHA peels for reasons of safety and reduced downtime.

The results of TCA peels are uniformly good, the risk of discoloration or excessively deep peeling is minimal, and both the procedure and recovery are fairly easily tolerated.

I typically employ 35-percent TCA peels for wrinkles around the lower eyelid area as part of a surgical rejuvenation. The down time is within the surgical recovery period, and dark circles and wrinkles are very much reduced, or eliminated.

Professionally performed AHA peels are more superficial and are performed in a series of treatments. In concentrations below 70-percent they are only marginally useful for the treatment of deep wrinkles. Thirty percent AHA peels administered by aestheticians cause some redness and flaking for a few days. Physician-applied 70-percent AHA peel causes severe reddening of the skin followed by flaking. The process takes about a week to subside, but is never as severe as the aftermath of TCA peels. AHA is very well tolerated and virtually complication-free but is reserved for the treatment of fine wrinkles, discolorations, and irregularities, and overall improvement of the condition and appearance of the skin. With the advent of the *Youth Corridor No Peel Peel*, all this has changed; 70-percent glycolic acid peels can be performed without discomfort or downtime, with excellent results. Here too, the peels are most effective when done in a series of six peels two to three weeks apart.

It is hard to predict how long after peeling fine wrinkles reappear. That is a function of individual skin and lifestyle, as was the case with the original wrinkles. The purpose of peeling is to reduce fine and deep wrinkles, even skin tones, and eliminate rough skin areas.

The cost of peels varies widely. AHA peels are fairly inexpensive, usually $250 to $350 per session. Deep peels performed under anesthesia can cost $2000 to $4000 or more for the deeper peels, depending on a number of variables.

MICRONEEDLING AND PRP

Microneedling is a relatively new addition to the list of effective antiaging, skin tightening, and skin repair tools. The concept is novel, and has proven its worth over several years of successful application. Numerous scientific papers have shown that tiny, shallow, micro-incisions into the skin heal invisibly and stimulate significant collagen production and skin tightening. This revelation has found numerous uses. In the Youth Corridor Clinic we use a hand-held, battery-driven device with sterile mini-blades to stamp hundreds of superficial micro-incisions into the skin. The procedure is not at all painful. Various collagen stimulating substances are spread on the skin before and after the microneedling, and these are driven into the dermis of the skin where they can stimulate collagen production. If you remember the discussion of vitamin C, I mentioned that the difficulty was in getting it into the skin. Microneedling expedites that process.

The entire process is quick and, depending on the depth of needling chosen, leaves little more than transient redness. Deeper needling, up to a depth of one millimeter, leaves mini-wounds that require up to forty-eight hours to heal and disappear. The collagen production and skin tightening begin immediately, and continues for weeks. Most patients report visible improvement in ten days. The process is repeated in monthly intervals, for at least three sessions.

The simple healing of the micro-wounds tightens and resurfaces the skin. Adding vitamin C aides the process, but the maximum effect can be achieved with the addition of Platelet Rich Plasma. Platelet Rich Plasma, or PRP is a concentration of naturally occurring growth factors in the blood. In the process a small amount of the patient's blood is drawn into sterile tubes, which are centrifuged to separate the plasma from the red blood cells, and concentrate the growth factors in the plasma. It is estimated that the concentration of these essential factors is increased tenfold by the process. The PRP is applied to the skin and the microneedling is performed, driving the collagen stimulating growth factors into the skin.

We have found this to be very effective, and very well tolerated. In twenty-four to forty-eight hours the area is completely healed, and makeup can be applied.

The procedure is useful to help tighten any skin area: face, neck, arms etc. It also used to correct collagen deficient areas like stretch marks and acne scars. Stretch marks are areas where the skin has stretched rapidly, and the collagen in the dermis has thinned. That accounts for the depression in the skin where it has been stretched, and healed with a thin layer of collagen. Virtually the same problem is found in skin pitted by acne. Acne pimples heal with a thin, depressed scar causing pock marks, or saucer like depressions. These problem are typically recalcitrant and don't respond to topical application of lotions, serums, or "miracle" stretch mark reducing products. The use of microneedling with PRP goes directly to the problem, and very significant improvement has been achieved in both conditions.

Microneedling fees vary between \$250 and \$500 per session. Fees for microneedling with PRP are between \$1250 and \$1500 per session.

Laser Wrinkle Removal, Skin Resurfacing and Tightening

One of the best and most modern treatments for surface wrinkles and skin irregularities is laser resurfacing. There are lots of different lasers, and it's a big, complicated topic. A laser—the acronym for Light Amplification by Stimulated Emission of Radiation—is focused high-energy light waves whose force is harnessed and finely directed by an integrated computer. Over the years, various types of lasers have been used in surgery. They vary from invasive and destructive to superficial. To avoid more confusion than is necessary, some processes that are not technically lasers will be considered in this section as well.

What Laser Treatment Can and Cannot Do.

The first thing to know is that the only way to remove skin-surface irregularities is by destroying them. Removing a blemish with a laser means directing the high-energy light beam onto the blemish for a fraction of a second and destroying it. The treated blemish or brown spot becomes darker, dries out and over a few days, flakes off, and disappears. This is how most lasers used in skin-care clinics work.

Physicians may also elect to destroy and remove the lesion more aggressively with the CO2 laser. This insures definitive and permanent removal but leaves the site raw for a period. Both methods work. The first takes multiple treatments but has less unsightly downtime. The point of this digression is to open the window to the many types of lasers available to do the same job.

Understanding that lasers are great for treatment of surface irregularities, let us look briefly at the lasers meant to tighten skin and remove wrinkles. Arguably, removing wrinkles effectively requires destroying the superficial, epidermal wrinkle and stimulating new, dermal collagen growth to thicken and firm the skin. And to some extent, the laser does the job. This is particularly true in specific areas where lasers are used to ablate, or destroy, wrinkles, such as the vertical lines in the upper lip. Loose, inelastic skin is also treated with lasers and laser-like instruments, in this case aiming the beam beneath the surface, directly into the dermis, and sparing the surface. The objective is to stimulate new collagen growth deep within the skin. The surface of the skin remains undamaged, and some new collagen forms over a period of months. There are some positive effects, but it remains to be seen how significant the cosmetic improvement actually is. We offer these skin tightening treatments in our clinic and have tried them on ourselves. I'm not convinced they work very well, but the jury is still out. Some of our most discerning patients are delighted with their own results.

Lasers are great for ablating, or removing, pigment, small vascular skin deformities, capillaries, age spots, superficial wrinkles, and unwanted hair. They are not as impressive as a treatment for sagging skin or deep wrinkles, and do very little to remove scars or stretch marks.

The first resurfacing laser in general use was the CO2 laser. The system is fitted with a pulsed control that allows it to deliver rapid and concentrated beams of light to the skin. The internal computer allows the depth of penetration to be accurately controlled. The pattern is coursed over a wrinkled skin area resulting in skin destruction to the papillary (highest level of the) dermis. This effectively wipes out the layer of skin containing the wrinkles while preserving the layer necessary for skin regeneration. The speed and accuracy of the procedure has made it an immensely popular tool. Theoretically, deep chemical peel should be equally effective in wrinkle ablation, but the reality is different. Depth of treatment cannot be accurately gauged other than with the computerized laser. It is the only treatment performed at the appropriate and uniform depth throughout. That allows for aggressive accuracy without worry of overly deep penetration. It is particularly valuable for treating specific wrinkles, such as vertical lip lines or creases in the thin skin of the lower eyelid, as well as for full-face resurfacing. The ability to accurately control treatment depth has made this a great tool. Results are superior and side effects fewer.

CO2 laser procedures are performed in the doctor's office. Both plastic surgeons and dermatologists offer the service. The area to be treated is injected with a local anesthetic, and the laser is patterned on the skin in a series of narrowly separated dots. This superficial layer of coagulated skin is wiped away with a moist gauze pad, and a second pass is made over or alongside the actual deep wrinkle. This, too, is wiped away, and an ointment is applied. The area is kept clean and moist, and new pink skin covers the treated area in about a week. At that point, cosmetics can be used for coverage. Six to eight weeks pass before normal skin color returns.

The areas where I have found the CO2 laser invaluable are the difficult to treat vertical lines in the upper lip, smile lines, and pigmented, wrinkled skin under the eyes. Years ago, I used the CO2 laser to treat smile lines alongside the eyes, but I find that Botox does the job better. Usually the best way to get rid of vertical lines in the upper lip is a combination of laser resurfacing and filling in the deep lines by means of a fat transfer. Total facial resurfacing with the CO2 laser is well-tolerated by individuals with fair skin, and quite effective. It is performed to treat generalized wrinkling, which is usually a problem associated with fair Northern European skin. CO2 laser treatment is more problematic with darker skin, as the treated area may lose too much pigment and be left with color irregularities. People with more skin pigment are better served by multiple, more superficial treatments using the less destructive lasers described later in this section. One of the positive uses of this side effect of depleting pigment is for removing the dark circles under the eyes. In this circumstance, loose lower lid skin and excess pigment add up to dark rings under the eyes. The CO_2 laser is used to resurface and de-pigment the skin, resulting in smoother, tighter, pigment-free under-eye skin.

Fractionated laser treatments, such as Fraxel, offer varied depth therapy for every type of skin resurfacing and tightening, with varying amounts of post-laser downtime. Most dermatologists and plastic surgeons choose the laser with which they have the most experience and best results.

As mentioned above, lasers used to tighten the skin do so by stimulating new collagen production. There are many new laser technologies that work in this fashion, including non-laser light sources and heat producing devices that concentrate energy in the dermis and stimulate collagen production, thereby tightening the skin. This effect is less than overwhelming, and transitory, and must be repeated to retain the effect. All these technologies work to some degree.

Lasers used to treat sunspots and superficial wrinkles and remove hair are part of the services offered by most skin-care centers. The most up-to-date lasers calibrate the patient's skin coloration based on the Fitzpatrick scale, to determine suitability for treatment and to establish proper settings on the onboard computer. Skin color and lesion color are important in laser settings since darker pigment absorbs the laser energy. The same holds true for laser hair removal, which is very successful for ablating dark hair, and far less so for lighter hair.

Laser and IPL procedures are usually performed by aestheticians or nurses, under the supervision of physicians, and are quite safe.

MICROSUCTION

Microsuction is a very effective and minimally invasive technique. Before I try to wiggle my way out of whether microsuction is minimally invasive, or just plain surgery, let me tell you what it means and what it does.

Microsuction is a term I began using some years ago to describe a form of liposuction using tiny specialized instruments for the treatment of particular facial problems. As you doubtless know, liposuction refers to the surgical removal of excess fat using a powerful suction apparatus and sterile steel tubes, called cannulas, which look something like long, thin drinking straws. Carrying that analogy further, the straws come in varied lengths and calibers (diameters), depending on the task to be performed. The cannulas used for liposuction on the hips or abdomen are typically four to five millimeters in diameter, or nearly one-quarter inch. Microsuction cannulas are usually vary from one and a half to three millimeters in diameter. Using these fine cannulas facilitates the controlled removal of limited amounts of fat in special areas about the face. The procedure was devised to deal with the tiny fat pouches that tend to develop alongside the corners of the mouth, the small accumulations of fat along the jawline and neck, and the heavy folds that develop along the nasolabial line from the corners of the nose to the corners of the mouth. Removing the fatty spots helps a lot, of course, but as a side benefit, the microsuction irritates the undersurface of the skin and seems to stimulate it to tighten and look better.

An area where this does wonders is the double chin. All levels of excess fat about the chin and neck will be improved, but those with the worst problem have the most impressive results. Usually a tiny incision is made under the chin, and a two- or three-millimeter cannula is inserted and the excess fat suctioned away. The result is so good that for some younger patients it can eliminate the need for neck-lift. That's possible, of course, but don't count on it. What you can be assured of is visible improvement. More often, this procedure is best for smaller areas and for individuals in their late thirties and forties whose skin retains a healthy elasticity. The least dramatic results are in those individuals with little excess fat but an anatomically obtuse angle between the neck and mandible (lower jaw). The sum of all this is that if the fatty accumulations along the jaw, and elsewhere, are dealt with early by microsuction, not only are they eliminated, but the skin over them tightens and adds to the result. Here, the sum is greater than its parts.

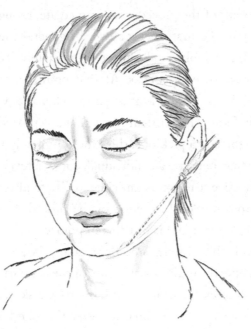

Fine microsuction catheter inserted behind earlobe and passed along jawline to treat jowls.

Often simply inserting the finest catheter from behind the earlobe, along the mandible, is all that is necessary to correct and tighten early loosening of the jawline. This is a minor procedure that delivers a quick, refreshing correction. It is not a substitute for surgery but sometimes is all that is necessary to deal with the situation. And for young people, it is better than surgery. Simple microsuction of the jawline and the pouches alongside the mouth should be considered whenever a patient is undergoing eyelid or other facial surgery. It is a disservice not to think of it, for so much can be gained so easily. The addition of microsuction of the jawline or mouth adds little to the operative time and nothing to recovery time, and it is a rare case in which I do not perform it as part of a face-lift. Microsuction alone is among the most popular options in fighting the early signs of aging.

Microsuction is performed under local anesthesia and sedation. A tiny hole is made either under the chin or behind the earlobes, through which the cannula is introduced. These sites are chosen because they make for easy access to the trouble spots, and they are not readily visible. The result of the procedure is immediate, though masked a bit by swelling over the first week or two. In general there is very little bruising, and you look good almost immediately. The actual result matures over six to eight weeks. At that point, all the swelling has gone and the skin is as taut as it is going to be. The procedure is very, very low-risk. I know better than to say that any procedure is risk-free, but if I were forced to pick one, this would probably be it. The major downside is that perhaps an individual, for whatever reason, doesn't have as impressive a result as anticipated. There also may be trauma to a nerve, from the local injection or the procedure itself. This is an exceedingly rare event and is usually temporary.

In general, this simple procedure takes about half an hour to perform and effectively eliminates some of the earmarks of early aging, refines the lower-face contours and tightens the skin; all this without traditional surgery, with minimal recovery time, and little or no risk. Sounds too good to be true, but for the appropriate patients it buys years of good looks and pushes the need for actual surgery years down the road. The cost for facial microsuction varies from $3500 to $6500, depending on the extent of treatment and whether it is being combined with other procedures.

KYBELLA

In 2015, Allergan, the company that owns Botox, spent $2.1B to acquire the company that produces Kybella, a product that dissolves fat. Kybella has only recently been generally available. It is, basically, a series of injections of a deoxycholic acid, meant to dissolve fat. Suggested use is the treatment of double chins. The substance is injected within a pattern under the jaw. From 12 to 24 injections is a normal range for each session. Up to six sessions are necessary, no less than a month apart. All patients report a reduction in submental fat (double chin), but there is no consensus on whether the result is smooth, and whether the skin tightens after the fat dissipates. There seems to be no reason to expect the skin to contract in any but the youngest patients. Since Kybella is relatively new to the market it is difficult to evaluate results beyond photographs provided by the manufacturer. The cost of a course of Kybella injections to reduce a double chin is estimated to be similar to the cost of microsuction. In this case, the trade-off would be numerous injections over a number of months versus a single, minimally invasive procedure.

CORRUGATOR RESECTION

The corrugators are a pair of tiny muscles that really leave their mark. These small bands are considered muscles of facial expression. They originate at the bony rim deep at the ends of the eyebrows and course horizontally to insert into the skin between the eyebrows over the bridge of the nose. When one is relaxed, they relax and there is no sign of their action. When one frowns or makes quizzical expressions, these little devils snap into action; the muscles contract, drawing the skin between the eyebrows together, and causing vertical furrows above the bridge of the nose. Everyone has them, and everyone can produce those furrows. Some of us have more active corrugator muscles, frown more frequently and strongly and produce permanent vertical lines etched into the skin between the eyebrows. Again, the repetitive action ultimately etches frown lines into the skin. This kind of action is a form of tensing the facial muscles, and you can see how facial muscle exercises can lead to wrinkles. These are among the earliest-appearing deep facial wrinkles and often stand conspicuously against an otherwise unlined forehead. They have the ability to impart a strained, tense countenance and are never flattering. Happily, there are two simple, effective, safe treatments.

Since the corrugator muscles serve only to produce those frown lines, and since other related muscles can continue to animate the brow, eliminating the corrugators would be no loss and a considerable gain. That is exactly what we do. Cutting the muscles eliminates the majority of the vertical frown lines, smooths the brow, and prevents the development of further lines. This has proven to be a simple, effective procedure and should be considered when one notices the gradual etching of these frown lines into the skin. The earlier the lines are dealt with, the better and more complete the result.

Vertical frown lines between the eyebrows caused by the action of the corrugator muscle.

Corrugator muscle resection can be performed under local anesthesia, or local anesthesia and sedation. I usually suggest sedation because people are anxious about someone fussing so near their eyes. Otherwise it is simple and quick and could easily be done under local anesthesia alone. A small incision is made in the natural skin fold of the upper lid, close to the nose. The length of the incision is about half an inch, and soon becomes virtually invisible. If the patient is having their eyes done, the corrugator procedure is performed at the same time, through the same upper-lid incision. It adds little extra time and no further discomfort to the procedure. The thin corrugator muscle is easily identified, and a tiny section is cut through it. The wound heals in a few days, and patients report no difficulty with expression. The vertical lines between the brows are greatly reduced or eliminated, and fat transplants may be used to iron out long-standing lines.

This is a very nice tool, since there is great physical improvement from so small a procedure. Something about a permanent scowl, or even the lines that suggest it, detracts greatly from an attractive face. This procedure can be the answer. Costs vary from $3500 to $4500, depending on the surgeon and what other procedures are being performed. Most often, corrugator resection is done with eyelid surgery, when an incision will be present in the area.

In truth, I think Botox injections are every bit as effective as dividing the corrugator muscles, sometimes more so. The problem, of course, is that Botox treatments are expensive and must be repeated every few months. But if you're a Botox user, a drop or two between the eyebrows does the job.

IMPLANT MATERIALS AND IMPLANTS

Cheeks and chins. There are all sorts of materials currently available as implants. A good many of them are space-age stuff, and some of the rest are old standbys, and all depend for success on creative judgment and good taste. Generally, facial implants are designed to fill in defects and increase proportions. Cheekbone and chin implants augment proportions and are permanent. They are made of vulcanized silicone or other well-tolerated substances. Implants are often employed in antiaging surgery, and can enhance the appearance of the jawline and take up a bit of slack skin. Cheek implants increase angularity, fill the skin, and produce an element of lift. Even aging, wrinkled skin looks better and less wrinkled when draped over graceful, high cheekbones or a strong chin. Angularity suits our concept of beauty, in part because it makes use of highlights and shadows. It accentuates what is good, drawing attention away from the rest. Years ago, when a face-lift was performed, cheekbone implants might be inserted on top of existing natural cheekbones to add angularity and increase the effect of the surgery. They provided a high point for draping the skin and took up slack. Today, the layered lifting procedures build up the cheekbone area, and, if necessary, additional fat is inserted in the area. Silastic cheekbone implants have become less popular, partially because of the high rate of complications, particularly slippage and malposition.

Chin implants are inserted on the prominence of the chin, under the vertical mentalis muscles, which run from the tip of the chin into the lower lip. The function of these muscles is to tense and roll out the lower lip, and as such they are important in speech. Chin implants can be inserted from inside the lip and slipped under the mentalis muscles or from an external incision under the chin and placed in the same position. The effect of a chin implant is immediately visible as a stronger jaw and more balanced profile. Chin implants hurt. The stretching of the mentalis muscles and the skin above them takes a few days to settle down, but the result is worth the trouble.

Fat grafting to cheeks and chin. As good, and as permanent as these implants can be, in most cases I much prefer to augment the areas with fat grafts. It's fast, painless, and trouble free. This is particularly effective in the cheek bone area, as described in the section on fat grafting. For modest chin enlargement fat transfer is often the procedure of choice. The injections are made directly into muscle, and the rich blood supply of the muscle insures excellent permanent take. When greater augmentation is necessary I rely on the old stand-by, silicone implants.

Implant material must be well tolerated by the body and not cause inflammatory reactions. They must be stable over time and relatively easy to use. Materials other than autologous substances, like bone, cartilage and fat, must be cleared by the FDA for medical use. Among the most frequently used are solid silicone rubber, known as Silastic, and polytetrafluoroethylene, known as Gore-Tex. There are others as well: AlloDerm is a popular soft implant material made of treated cadaver skin. It often serves as a filler for lip enhancement and is also layered in sheets to build up deficient contours, or cover implants.

Silastic, in its solid form, is used in joint replacement, artificial heart valves, as the envelope in breast implants and for chin and cheek implants, among many other uses. It is extremely well tolerated, doesn't shrink, doesn't set up significant inflammation and has been used successfully for more than fifty years. Silastic should not be confused with liquid silicone used as an injectable filler. There is a long and tragic history of silicone injections, its misuse and the awful complications resulting from it. Small droplets of pure liquid silicone were among the first substances used as filler. Unfortunately, the silicone often moved from the intended site, and since it was permanent and proved extremely difficult to remove, there were many problems. Use of silicone as a tissue filler was banned, but off-label use continued, often with good results. Only the bad results got attention, and horrible misadventures were not uncommon. Some of the black-market silicone was terribly impure and caused inflammation. When the impure substance was injected into breasts to enlarge them, infections, granulomas, and skin and breast loss resulted. For the most part, injection of silicone, pure or impure, has almost disappeared.

Gore-Tex is similar to Teflon. It, too, has been used for many years and many purposes, including vascular grafts. For facial enhancement, it is provided in many forms and is popular for filling in the nasolabial folds and for lip enhancement. It is well tolerated by the body and is permanent. Like Silastic, Gore-Tex implants can be removed, if necessary. When used in the lips, the substance can often be readily felt, giving an unnatural result. I am not a fan of its use. Still, it is well thought of by many plastic surgeons, is safe, and has a place among the implant options.

ELEVEN

Correction

This is the section devoted to correction of already visible signs of aging. It is impossible to accurately pinpoint when these symptoms require correcting. And certainly not at what age specific steps should be taken. My philosophy is that we should deal with the mirror and not the calendar. We all age at our own pace, depending on how well we care for ourselves, and on our genetic makeup. When the signs of aging appear, we each must decide whether we feel they are appropriate, unsightly, or somewhere in between. The decision to seek corrective measures to reverse the signs of aging is a purely personal matter. Giving you an honest overview of what is possible is part of the mission of this book.

BLEPHAROPLASTY

Blepharoplasty is the medical term for cosmetic eyelid surgery, usually one of the earliest sought and most frequently performed procedures. The name comes from *bleph*, pertaining to the eyelids, and *plasty*, to mold: to mold the eyelids—a genteel way of describing the procedure. In reality, it amounts to surgically removing the excess skin on and about the lids and correcting baggy, tired-looking eyes.

Blepharoplasty is an astoundingly popular procedure performed some three-hundred-thousand times yearly in the United States. The fact that the result of the surgery is usually excellent and the procedure easily tolerated accounts for the popularity it enjoys. As an antiaging surgical procedure, it is among the earliest performed, typically in one's mid-forties but increasingly earlier. That should come as no surprise, since the skin of the eyelids is the thinnest and most delicate of the face. The eyelids provide an actual mirror of the system and swell at the slightest provocation. Here one finds the first signs of allergy, illness, emotional distress, or the results of last night's spicy food and alcohol. Repeated cycles of swelling—and the rubbing that unconsciously follows—take a toll on the elasticity of the eyelids. When the fine, thin, skin is subjected to regular abuse, there can be no surprise in its distortion and the breakdown of elasticity. Each smile etches lines on the outside corners of the eyes, as does each squint to block the sun or look off into the distance. We do squint, and we do like to smile and laugh, and the damage piles up.

With the natural loss of elasticity, the eyebrows drop a bit, adding excess tissue to the upper lids. The fat pads of the lower lids become more prominent, and bags develop. For some this is a congenital problem seen as early as the teen years; for most, it develops considerably later. The bags, or puffs, under the eyes cast a shadow on the ring of skin beneath them, and soon the dark circles of the under trough are added to the brew. At some point in the process, one says, "Enough."

The signs of aging of the eyelids, which took years to develop, takes but an hour to correct. The operation is most often performed in a private clinic or ambulatory-surgery facility. It is generally agreed that hospitalization and general anesthesia are unnecessary in all but the most unusual circumstances. Prior to surgery, preoperative photographs are taken in the standing position for comparison to the intra-operative appearance in the recumbent position. Lying down, one's face appears free of the pull of gravity and many problems disappear. When the two realities are integrated, the excess skin of the upper lids is outlined in indelible ink, the patient sedated and local anesthetic is injected into the upper and lower lid areas. Marking is not usually necessary on the lower lid, as the incision site is determined by the skin crease just below the lower lashes. The excess skin of the upper lids, which has been marked, is excised along with the tissue beneath it. Fat pockets that cause puffiness of the upper lid are identified and removed. This is particularly important at the inside corner of the eye, where increasing fullness develops over the years. If the patient is at some stage of developing vertical frown lines between the brows, the corrugator muscles that cause the frown are dealt with through the same incision. The upper-lid skin is then closed with a fine nylon suture, which is woven invisibly under the skin, sticking out like a cat's whisker at either end. These are removed three or four days later. There are other ways to accomplish this, including individual visible sutures or even skin glue. Techniques vary, with the common goal of producing a fine and virtually invisible line.

The lower lid is operated on through an incision immediately below the lashes, usually in a tiny wrinkle line. It heals rapidly and well, and signs of incision are all but gone within weeks of surgery. After the lower-lid incision is made, a number of variations are possible. One technique is employed if the problem is purely wrinkled skin, another if it is puffiness more than wrinkles. To treat wrinkles, the skin itself is separated from the muscle below, the pockets of excess fat may be removed through small incisions in the muscle, and the skin is trimmed and re-draped in a wrinkle-free but natural manner.

If the primary focus is puffiness under the eyes, then the culprits are the pockets of excess fat. This is often causes a deep trough beneath the puffy area. The muscle beneath the skin is incised without being separated from the skin. This skin-and-muscle flap affords excellent access to the fat pockets and the trough below. Some excess fat may be removed, but largely it is relocated into the trough, making the entire under-eye area smooth. Aggressive fat removal can lead to a hollow under-eye look, and has largely been abandoned. The skin and muscle are trimmed and the incision closed with a fine sutures.

When the skin-and-muscle flap is employed, the lower-eyelid skin retains its nourishment from the muscle below, and it is safe to perform a peel or laser resurfacing at the same time. That helps remove fine wrinkles and dark circles below the eyes. When the situation dictates use of the skin flap technique, laser or peeling is not employed for fear of damaging the already thin skin.

There are numerous minor complications associated with eyelid surgery. The most common is some degree of dry eye or alteration in production and quality of tears. This temporary situation occurs in more than 75 percent of cases and almost always resolves spontaneously. All patients are treated with artificial tears to prevent this discomfort. In a few cases, this is a longer-lasting problem. Other circumstances, such as irritation and swelling of the conjunctiva covering the eye, may cause the lower lid to stand away from the eye. This is an annoying but treatable problem. A more serious but far less frequent problem is overaggressive skin removal, which may result in drooping of the lower lid. These cosmetic complications are unpleasant but can usually be satisfactorily resolved. Rarely, among the millions of blepharoplasties performed, there is undetected, significant bleeding behind the eye, which can cause blindness if left untreated. Though most surgeons may never incur this complication, they are always on the lookout for it so that the exceedingly rare case can be properly dealt with. Excessive upper-lid skin removal can result in an inability to fully close the eyes at rest. This usually resolves with time and the pull of gravity, which bring the upper lid down, whether we want it to or not.

There are other problems related to blepharoplasty that are beyond the scope of this brief look, and again, most are easily dealt with. The best way to avoid problems is to be aware that they are possible. Dealing with the variables of healing makes every situation unique. Having performed thousands of these procedures over the years, it is clear to me that a combination of knowledge, experience, and common sense is essential to achieve the best possible result. It is a popular procedure because it is good and it is safe.

The procedure, as performed in the ambulatory surgery suite, takes about an hour. Sedation and local anesthesia are used. The patient sleeps through the procedure, and the surgery is very well-tolerated. Postsurgical treatment includes twenty-four hours of iced compresses, which control swelling, discoloration, and pain. Most patients don't need analgesics after the first night, if at all. Sutures are removed on the third or fourth day. By the end of the week, swelling and discoloration have subsided and eye makeup may be worn. Fees for upper- and lower-lid blepharoplasty performed together range from $10000 to $15000.

A properly performed eye-lift, with or without associated procedures, will remove years of wear and tear and restore a lively youth to the central part of your face.

Excess skin of the upper eyelids is marked and removed.

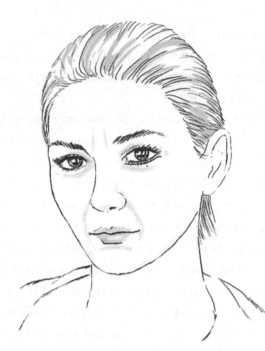

The lower-eyelid incision is made immediately below the eyelashes. No lashes are cut.

CLAMPING EYELID WRINKLES

This simple procedure achieves a lot and is among the quickest fixes of all. It is directed at the patient with excess, wrinkled lower-eyelid skin. Stand in front of the mirror and smile a few times. If the skin under your eyes doesn't fall back in place but forms tiny folds and wrinkles, then you see the problem. This is primarily a condition of middle age, though young people with years of sun exposure also exhibit the signs. The small folds of skin are anesthetized and gently lifted away from the underlying muscle. This is easily done without distorting the eyelid. A fine clamp is used to pinch the excess skin, which is then precisely excised with fine scissors. There is no bleeding, and the incision is closed with fine sutures that are removed in three-four days. There is virtually no postoperative swelling or discomfort, and by the end of the week there is little sign of surgery except for the absence of the excess skin. The resulting scar is just beneath the margin of the lid, and heals nearly invisibly.

The skin clamping can be used with any number of other procedures and is often employed as a touch-up for people who have had their eyes done in the past. Complications are rare, and recovery is swift. Fees average in the $5000 range. This is a case of achieving a lot for very little in terms of discomfort and time.

A fine clamp is used to "pinch off" the excess skin of the lower lid.

TRANS-CONJUNCTIVAL BLEPHAROPLASTY

Another mouthful. This is an operation usually restricted to young adults. It treats puffy, baggy lower eyelids in people without loose skin or wrinkles. That eliminates all but those in their twenties or thirties who have suffered through youth with people saying, "You look tired. Is anything wrong?" No, there's nothing wrong. You look tired because you have inherited excess fat beneath the muscle of your lower lids. It's a family trait. Have a look at the family album. It's there—and it's easy to get rid of.

The term *subconjunctival,* or *transconjunctival, blepharoplasty* means that the actual surgery is done through the inner lining, the conjunctiva, of the eyelid and no visible, external skin incision is necessary. Under local anesthesia and sedation, the eyelid is held down and the cornea protected. An incision is made in the eyelid lining, or conjunctiva, in order to reach the fat pockets just deep to it, so the operation is sub, or deep to, the conjunctiva. After the fat is removed, some ointment may be put over the area, and the eye is allowed to close. No sutures are necessary, and healing is rapid and invisible. Usually, some temporary bruising and discoloration result, but otherwise there is no sign of surgery.

Young people with puffy lower lids are good candidates for subconjunctival blepharoplasty.

The procedure is specifically designed for people with excess fatty bags but no loose skin or wrinkles. When the fat is removed, the skin becomes less tense, and soon contracts. This is usually the procedure of choice for younger people whose skin is elastic and will shrink readily after the fat is removed. If one's lower eyelid skin is loose already or very inelastic, this procedure alone may be inappropriate; however, in some cases laser resurfacing of the eyelid skin can be done at the same time. This tightens the lower-eyelid skin and removes blemishes and pigment. Some surgeons follow the sub-conjunctival portion with excision of a strip of skin.

Fees are in the $5000 to $8500 range.

TEAR TROUGH FILLING

The tear trough is the deep semi-circle under the eyes that often takes on a dark cast and makes one seem tired and dissipated. It is usually associated with some element of puffiness above, which accentuates the trough. Simply filling the tear trough with hyaluronic acid filler, or fat, can totally reverse the problem. Using hyaluronic acid filler is simple and fast, and can be done under local or topical anesthesia in an office visit, but the result is temporary. The procedure must be performed by an experienced professional, and care must be taken in placement and volume of filler used.

Autologous fat transfer requires sedation or local anesthesia, and usually provides permanent correction. The procedure is a delicate one and must be done with great care. Patients see immediate, gratifying results, and the procedure has become increasingly popular.

LIMITED-INCISION FACE-LIFT TECHNIQUE (L.I.F.T.), SHORT-SCAR FACE-LIFT, OR MODERN MINI-LIFT

There is no such thing as a "one size fits all" face-lift. Surgical techniques should address specific problems, and the same procedure is not applicable to every problem and every person. As a plastic surgeon with a long-standing interest in anti-aging surgery, I have always sought the simplest, least invasive route to meet my patient's goals. A forty-nine-year-old woman does not have the same aging issues as a sixty-seven-year-old, so why should she be offered the same operation? Men want to tidy up their necks and have their skin fit. Women are concerned with wrinkles, folds, and blemishes. Why would I offer them the same single option? It doesn't make sense.

It has always been clear to me that if we are to provide a full range of corrective options, something must fill the void between simple, noninvasive skin treatments and a full face-lift. As we have already noted, visible facial aging begins around the eyelids. But soon a generalized and increasingly noticeable loss of elasticity begins. It may be manifested by fleshiness along a formerly clean jawline and deepening of the nasolabial folds. There is loss of cheekbone angularity, some loosening of the skin beneath the neck, or perhaps a bit of a double chin. All this begins to appear in the mid-to-late-forties; earlier for fine-skinned, fair individuals, later for the thicker-skinned and darker-complexioned. For most people, these changes signify the passage from youth. They are not warmly welcomed, nor are they significant enough to elicit thoughts of a face-lift. They are too new and not yet overwhelming. A steady despair and resignation sets in, and there seems to be nothing to do but watch and wait.

Even if a road map of facial wrinkles has not yet appeared, some relief would be welcome. It is possible to stop the progress in a young person before the changes have pushed her from youthful to matronly. Clean up the jawline, return the cheekbone prominence to what it used to be and undo those nasolabial folds along the cheeks and lines beside the mouth. While these changes are not terrible, they are beyond the scope of injections, lasers and peels.

In the past, the most common advice was, "Wait and do a face-lift when you are ready." Few plastic surgeons, myself included, thought very much of doing less. We were taught that anything less than a full face-lift wasn't worth doing. We were wrong. Even as the nuances of the surgery and the sophistication of the profession advanced, we held to preconceived notions. But I was searching for a better solution; one that could be applied earlier, produce a natural result and make the early-middle-aged patient look appealingly young again.

It was at that point, in the mid-1980s, that I first encountered the rudiments of the S-lift, so named for its lazy-S incision. While visiting European colleagues, my host in Germany demonstrated a procedure that utilized only half the usual face-lift incision, and no incision behind the ears or on the neck. It was a far less extensive procedure than I was accustomed to. The patients recovered quickly, and the immediate results were impressive. I took the idea home, and after some years of tinkering, only the basic incision remained the same. My version of the S-lift could best be called a two-layer anterior face-lift. It is designed for the earlier stages of facial loosening; it tightens the skin and underlying muscle, effectively lifting everything from under the under chin area to the forehead. My associates and I soon considered this the procedure of choice to correct early jowls, loosening of the cheeks and deepening nasolabial folds. The idea of eliminating the incision on the neck was revolutionary. Women could wear their hair up without worrying about the visible, ugly scar.

A few years later, I reduced the incision further, eliminating the component in the scalp and increasing effectiveness. The result was even more natural. It corrected all loss of elasticity and drooping from the eyes above to the Adam's apple area below, and dramatically reduced the nasolabial fold. This was the limited-incision face-lift technique, or short-scar face-lift. It seemed to be exactly what surgeons and patients were looking for and became enormously popular. As with everything in medicine, many people have simultaneous inspiration, and one cannot lay claim to "inventing" a procedure. To paraphrase an old proverb, "Success has many authors; failure is an orphan." This modern mini-lift has been adopted, renamed, and publicized by many surgeons. The June 4, 2009, *New York Times* published a long article about the marketing of specialized face-lifts, making reference to the seminal importance of my original S-lift and the procedures it had spawned. But be warned: A new name doesn't make a new procedure. After the peer reviewed journal, *Aesthetic Surgery* published our scientific paper on the first 1000 limited-incision face-lifts performed by me, I smiled at advertisements for surgeons claiming credit for the new operation. I am happy to have had something to do with devising and popularizing an excellent procedure, but the real beneficiaries are my patients, who understood that the new procedure would help them achieve and maintain a natural, youthful appearance.

In order to understand how all this works, let's consider the anatomy of the face, what we are trying to achieve, and the difference between face-lift procedures.

The skin of the face lies on a bed of subcutaneous fat and wispy connective tissue. Only in areas of facial expression is it bound directly to the underlying muscles. That means that there are muscle-skin connections around the eyes, lips, mouth, nose and chin, but the entire cheek and neck area, from the ears to the nasolabial fold, is free of these attachments and not closely bound to the underlying tissues. Therefore, it is easily separated and lifted. It is because of this lack of firm anchors that these areas are liable to become lax and droop as soon as the skin begins to lose elasticity. Correcting that laxity, along with the tightening of the underlying tough muscle fascia, lends itself to successful repair, or lifting. This tough layer, called the subcutaneous muscular aponeurosis, or SMAS, is where much of the real pulling takes place, not the skin. This tightening helps alleviate jowls and deep nasolabial folds, and adds longevity to the result. The thin, flat platysma muscle, a continuation of the SMAS, which underlies the skin of the neck, is also tightened to correct the two loose bands under the chin.

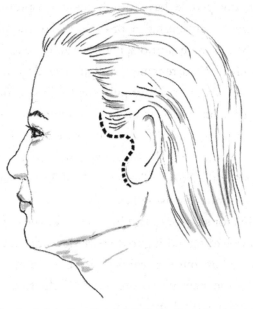

The incision for the L.I.F.T. No hair is shaved.

The limited-incision face-lift incision, or short-scar face-lift incision, begins in the bottom hair follicles of the sideburn and follows the path into the ear, behind the tragus, that little piece of cartilage that sticks out from the ear, and ends just behind the ear lobe. Signs of surgery disappear quickly, and one can confidently appear in public ten days after surgery. There is no scar behind the ears or on the neck, and women can wear their hair up without worrying about the noticeable signs of traditional face-lifts. Because the top of the incision is in the sideburn, there is no unsightly, telltale distortion of the hairline. The L.I.F.T. reverses the loss of elasticity that has caused facial sagging, and results in a firm, straight jawline. Ancillary procedures include microsuction of the double-chin area and corners of the mouth and fat transfers to lip lines, lips, cheekbones, and chin. Eyelid surgery is done at the same time, when indicated. The operation is particularly suited to the younger patient, and least effective against the road map of wrinkles often seen on the skin of older women. For this problem, other solutions apply.

Surgeons around the country are offering variations of this procedure to their patients, with equally rewarding results. The L.I.F.T. takes less than two hours to perform. It is usually performed under sedation and local anesthesia, corrects loose jowls, reduces nasolabial folds, loose neck skin, and reconstitutes the angularity of the cheekbone area. It does not correct the very lowest portion of the neck or the forehead. For these problems other variations of the face-lift may be used. After surgery the patient is wrapped in a helmet of gauze and elastic, which remains in place for forty-eight hours. No drains are used. Patients are encouraged to get up and walk around the next morning, and shower and wash their hair after forty-eight hours. There is virtually no pain or discomfort in the postoperative period. Maximum swelling occurs at seventy-two hours and quickly abates thereafter. Recovery time from the L.I.F.T. is less than for the traditional face-lift, and most people are back to work in ten days.

Fees for this procedure range from $15000 to $20000.

The S-lift differs from the L.I.F.T. only in the upper aspect of the incision, which in the case of the S-Lift curves like an S into the scalp. This aspect of the incision is necessary to lift and smooth forehead and temporal wrinkles. Like the limited-incision face-lift, the S-lift is performed in the private clinic or ambulatory-surgery facility under deep sedation and a local anesthetic. Just hearing the word "*local*" usually elicits the following statement.

"I don't want to hear anything or feel anything."

This is not an unreasonable response, but the level of sedation provided by the anesthesiologist is deep enough for patients to sleep through the entire procedure, while the local provides the actual anesthesia. There should be no discomfort and no memory of the procedure itself. More important, the safety level of this sort of anesthesia is excellent. It allows the patient to breathe unassisted and makes the immediate postoperative recovery very smooth—usually more so than after full general anesthesia, particularly avoiding the need for an endotracheal breathing tube. There is a time and place for general anesthesia, and it should be chosen according to the procedure, patient and circumstances.

C-LIFT

The C-lift is a cousin of the Limited Incision Facelift Technique. We began offering this least invasive operation to men some ten years ago. It gained wide acceptance in my practice for a number of reasons. Most men are concerned primarily with jowls and loosening skin under the jawline and neck. When dealing with men, several anatomical differences from women must be respected. Men have beards, and a natural hairless strip of skin between the beard and the ear. This must not be violated or the result is unnatural…and there is nothing more unacceptable than that.

A small C-shaped incision within the sideburn, sometimes extending into a natural crease for an inch or so, is all that is needed to gain access to the underlying Platysma muscle, and the strong SMAS fibers. Tightening these relieves the nasolabial folds, and eliminates jowls and upper neck laxity. Redundant skin is removed and the scar is hidden in the sideburn. A small incision is also made under the jaw to remove skin and help tighten the muscles. Recovery is quick, and signs of surgery are extremely minimal.

Fees for C-lift are between $12500 and $17500.

TRADITIONAL FACE-LIFT

In this operation, the skin is separated from the underlying tissues on the forehead, face, and neck, virtually from temple to collarbones. The operation is designed to deal with more severe skin aging in the form of extensive wrinkling or laxity and loose lower neck, hence the greater extent of surgery than with the L.I.F.T. or S-lift. The underlying muscle fascia is tightened, as well as the thin platysma muscle layer of the neck.

The operation is usually performed in the private clinic or ambulatory surgery facility. There is really little need for hospitalization. The recovery period is a bit longer than for the S-lift and varies between ten days and two weeks. Blepharoplasty and microsuction are usually performed at the same time, and bruising and swelling last more than a week. Possible complications of all face-lift surgery include hematoma—a collection of blood under the skin that must be drained—and a host of other problems that are usually self-limited or easily corrected. This is true of the other, less-invasive face-lift variations but appreciably less frequently seen. The most dreaded possible complication is injury to the nerve that animates the face. It is a very rare complication indeed, and most surgeons will not see it in a lifetime of practice. In general, the operation is very safe and very successful. Everything depends on the skill of the surgeon, the appropriate choice of procedure, and the motivation of the patient. A variation of the face-lift and the ancillary procedures performed with it represent the most forceful option to undo a lifetime of aging and damage to the face. The point of our Youth Corridor program is to keep you from ever needing this surgery; but intervention at any point resets the clock and salvages many good years.

Fees are in the $17500 to $20000 range.

NECK LIFT

This procedure is directed at laxity of the skin of the neck in the absence of other signs of aging. Such circumstances are rare, and most patients find that they are focusing on the neck without realizing that loss of elasticity starts at the top and works its way down. Gravity doesn't pick just the neck; however, sometimes the loose, wrinkled neck skin is out of proportion with other changes. The neck lift involves an incision behind the ear and along the hairline. The neck skin is lifted up entirely from ear to ear and tightened. Microsuction is performed at the same time. The downside of the procedure is that the scar in the hairline behind the ear is sometimes noticeable, and no laxity above the jaw is corrected. Still, under proper circumstances it is a useful operation.

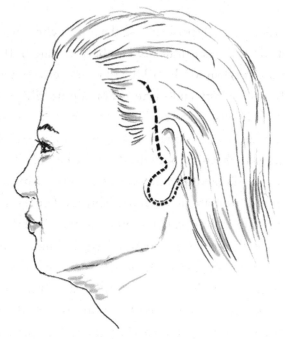

The traditional face-lift incision.

Men very often seek neck lift alone. There is very little that detracts from a man's youthful appearance than a "turkey wattle" neck. There are many surgical solutions varying from local excision through a small incision under the chin, to a full face and neck lift. Most often the problem is dealt with directly. The most common approach is through a horizontal incision under the chin. This allows removal excess fat and tightening of the loose bands of the platysma muscle. In more extreme cases the excess skin and loose muscle are directly removed through a "Z" like vertical incision. This procedure produces a longer, prominent scar, which fades to near invisibility, but it offers near total correction of the problem.

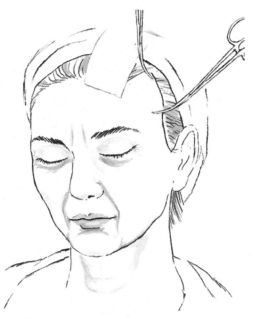

Direction of lift in traditional face-lift.

Many factors help determine the proper approach; not the least of which is understanding what the patient wants to achieve. Men and women have a decidedly different end point of surgery in mind, and that is surely a consideration. Over the years I have performed the Z-plasty neck lift for film stars, who required "skin that fits," as well as microsuction and a minor skin incision for business men who sought only an improvement.

TWELVE

CASE
STUDIES

This section of the book serves to demonstrate how the information covered in the text is applied to life situations of hypothetical patients. The cases represent a wide range of familiar problems. Some will apply to you, some a bit far afield. In the final section you will be able to find your own place in the scheme. Let's share a few examples—and remember, this is about the whole regime, not just an invitation to a face-lift. In every case the Youth Corridor strategy of *Prevention, Maintenance, and Correction* is applied.

At the Youth Corridor Clinic every patient is evaluated in the manner you will see described. Each patient is provided with an explicit, written report, a prescribed skin care routine, appropriate treatment products, a menu of appropriate corrective measures, and most importantly, a clear outline of what the next five years of normal aging will bring, and how they should be dealt with. A written and photographic record is maintained to document changes and progress, and a long-term strategy is provided in an organized and complete fashion.

In the absence of direct consultation and care, these case studies and the aging "map" to follow will illustrate the program, and do much to help you help yourself and remain in the Youth Corridor throughout adult life.

NANCY

Nancy is a thirty-five year-old woman. She was married for several years, is now divorced, has no children, currently lives in the Northeast, and works in the financial services industry. Her ancestry is English and German; she has fair skin and light-brown hair; she is five-feet-six-inches tall and weighs 120 pounds. Nancy leads an active life. She skis, plays tennis, and attends an aerobics class three times a week. Although she believes she still looks young, she has recently noticed a few smile lines around her eyes, which don't quite disappear when the smile does. The vertical lines between her eyebrows seem deeper after each day's work, though they are less noticeable when she has a little tan.

Nancy has frown lines between her eyes and early smile lines.

Nancy is concerned with the changes in her appearance and is determined to take appropriate steps to control matters before they steal her youth.

The Prescription

For a young, fair-skinned woman, sun exposure is a costly indulgence. Nancy is seeing the first signs of heritage, lifestyle, and time, and is in transition between the stages of prevention and correction. Here the Youth Corridor program will undo the signs of aging and establish a preventive routine.

Prevention

More careful sun protection is a must for fair-skinned individuals, as the single most potent action to prevent accelerated aging and skin cancer. In addition to rigorous use of sunscreen, *Youth Corridor Ultimate Antioxidant C Boost* should become part of a daily routine. This will help undo sun damage, protect against future damage, build collagen, and equalize skin tones.

Maintenance

Nancy's situation is typical for people in their early to mid-thirties. Her issues fall somewhere between Maintenance and Correction. And remember, even at this stage Prevention of further damage is key.

Visible issues are early frown lines and smile lines. The simplest treatment is Botox every four to six months. This will eliminate the lines and prevent etching further lines in the area, while allowing normal facial expression. The vertical lines between the eyebrows should be treated once or twice with fat transfers, which can permanently eliminate the ingrained folds or lines.

Accumulated sun damage, both visible and hidden, will require a series of AHA peels, like the *No Peel Peel* to revitalize her skin and begin the process of collagen rebuilding. These will be scheduled two weeks apart to allow the skin to return to normal between applications. They will serve to smooth the skin surface and reduce fine wrinkles, blotches and scaly areas, and help build collagen. Daily topical applications of penetrating vitamin C and E serum will be used to help undo the photo damage and restore the integrity of the dermal collagen.

Exercise

Beyond thirty years of age, high-impact aerobic exercise should be discontinued. Stop running. Substitute a low-impact program of bicycling, elliptical training, stair climbing, or swimming. All sports are encouraged. Outdoor activities require sunscreen pretreatment and regular reapplication. Waterproof and water-resistant varieties are especially valuable for those indulging in active sports.

Nutrition

Since there have been no great weight changes, Nancy is obviously aware of her personal caloric balance. Assuming that this is achieved with an appropriate, healthy diet containing regular portions of raw and lightly cooked vegetables, few supplements are required. Although fruit, vegetables, whole grains, and complex carbohydrates provide the backbone of this diet, protein and unsaturated fats such as olive oil should be encouraged. Lycopene is an antioxidant found in abundance in tomatoes, carrots, and other vegetables and fruits. It may be the most powerful of the dietary antioxidants and is said to play a role in cardiovascular health. It very likely has a positive effect on skin as well and should be included in a healthy diet. Antioxidants such as green tea are also encouraged.

Skin Care

A fair-skinned individual reporting scaly areas and early wrinkles has dry skin. Nancy's skin, so elegant in the past, is now at risk for early aging. She must do what she can to revitalize her skin and lessen wrinkles. It is still possible to prevent, or at least postpone, the changes that will require surgical correction. The Youth Corridor routine should become part of her daily life.

Morning: Shower and wash with mild soap or a gentle cleanser, followed by refreshing cool water rinse. Apply six to eight drops of *Youth Corridor Ultimate Antioxidant C Boost* serum to clean skin. Apply moisturizer or moisturizer/sunscreen SPF 30 combination as a daily routine. The moisturizer/sunscreen combination used, or the individual products chosen, must feel pleasant and soothing. Stinging or irritation is an invitation to try another product. Makeup may be applied as usual. Cosmetics containing sunscreen are not nearly as effective and are not a substitute. When time is spent at outdoor activities, the sunscreen must be replenished.

Evening: Wash with cleanser and warm water, then cool splash. This will remove makeup and the environmental and cellular debris of the day. Apply *Youth Corridor Retinultimate* gel to smile lines around eyes and cheeks, followed by soothing moisturizer. Continue this routine nightly. Use AHA exfoliant three weeks out of four, to give skin a rest period. Exfoliants in the form of moisturizers with low concentration AHA work slowly, not unpleasantly, but not adequately. An alternative is an exfoliating mask like *Youth Corridor Beta Hydroxy Mask.* There are many masks containing AHAs and BHAs, and all are very effective exfoliants. I usually suggest a monthly professional exfoliating peel, but this is not truly necessary with all the good home exfoliating options available.

Eye cream with peptides or AHA should be used around eyes every evening. No need to follow eye cream with moisturizer in the under-eye area, basically, that's what eye cream is…a potent moisturizer for the thin, easily damaged and easily wrinkled skin of the eye area.

Youth Corridor Antioxidant C Boost serum can be used in the evening instead of morning. Whatever suits your lifestyle, but remember, only once a day.

Supplements

Daily: No vitamin supplements are required if proper nutrition is maintained; 1000 mg of vitamin C, 800 IU of vitamin D are optional.

Evidence of the effectiveness of dietary antioxidant supplements is not convincing.

Summary

This is an active young woman with a genetic predisposition to early aging, and has accelerated the process with sun exposure. She has already seen the first hint of things to come in the form of deepening smile lines, vertical frown lines and irregularities of the skin surface, blotchiness, or discoloration. The treatment and maintenance program outlined is specifically designed to reverse present damage, maintain what hasn't been damaged, and prevent further accelerating the aging process. A woman entering the maintenance loop at this point will achieve visibly positive results of a subtle and gradual nature. That, after all, is what we are seeking. She is unlikely to need to alter this routine for several years, and will not likely need intervention for years to come.

We cannot stop the clock completely, but we can certainly reset it and slow it down.

PATRICIA

Patricia is forty-seven years old; born and raised in sunny southern California. Throughout high school and college and during her early working years, Patricia spent every possible moment in the surf and on the beach. Her Mediterranean heritage allowed for quick tanning without the painful sunburn her friends endured. Her skin had been slightly oily as a teenager, but she was never bothered with acne. In the twenty-five years since college, she has raised two children, returned to work as an advertising copywriter, gained and lost more than ten pounds almost every year and has finally resumed exercising. She uses sunscreen when she remembers, and has had very little time to devote to herself. Although she has never been a heavy smoker, and doesn't smoke at home, she has never given up the habit. Though mostly wrinkle-free, Patricia has noticed vertical lines in her upper lip, which are more noticeable with lipstick. She has become a little jowly and there is even a hint of a double chin, seemingly less fat than loosening skin. Previously, all this disappeared when she got down to her fighting weight. Now that she has kept most of the weight off for a year, her skin hasn't shrunk the way it always did in the past. For the first time, Patricia is beginning to see her face change, and she doesn't like it.

Patricia has vertical lines on her upper lip and some loose skin.

The Prescription

Patricia has been blessed with thick, moist skin that doesn't wrinkle easily and appears perennially tan. Even though her naturally dark pigment helps protect her skin from burning, it does not prevent the accelerated destruction of elastin and collagen fibers caused by ultraviolet rays. The loss of elasticity and loosening of facial skin has been markedly hastened by the sun. Thirty years of moderate smoking—and for a forty-seven year old who started a ten cigarette a day habit at seventeen, it has actually been thirty years—has also taken a toll. Although her skin type has thus far protected her from damage in the form of fine wrinkles, a natural consequence of the small blood vessel damage from smoking, the actual physical act of smoking cigarettes, the repetitive lip-pursing motion, has folded the vertical lines into her lips. It is not unusual for the upper lip to be worse than the lower, but both soon become pleated; the lines are accentuated by lipstick. What must take place here is reeducation, correction, and a maintenance routine.

The loose skin of the jowls and under the chin area is ideally suited for a mini-lift, or limited-incision face-lift. Before any surgery can be performed, Patricia must stop smoking for six weeks. Blood vessel constriction resulting from smoking cigarettes creates a unique risk of skin damage and scarring at surgery. The side benefit after surgery is that continued abstinence promotes better blood supply and healthier skin. Patricia has excess upper-eyelid skin, which will be dealt with at the same time. Her lip lines require laser resurfacing and fat transfer, also performed at the same time. The process of CO_2 laser resurfacing is a week in the healing and another month to six weeks before normal color is restored. For someone with dark, suntanned skin, there is always the danger of permanent pigment loss.

For this reason superficial resurfacing is performed, and may need to be repeated. Alternatively, Patricia will have tiny amounts of fat injected in the lip lines at the time of surgery. This will restore the deep loss. After recovery she can begin microneedling with PRP for the lip lines. This will help restore collagen and reduce the superficial lip lines.

She will need Botox twice yearly to treat her smile lines. There is every reason to believe that *Youth Corridor Ultimate Antioxidant C Boost* will undo much of the existing sun damage, and it is imperative to use it daily in addition to sunscreen to prevent further damage.

These procedures will undo most of the grossly visible damage, and leave Patricia with clean facial angles, skin that fits, and she'll be relatively free of lip lines. She has been able to erase ten years of aging and must now assume responsibility for maintaining her renewed youthful good looks.

Exercise

Patricia has finally managed to stabilize her weight. She has stopped smoking as a preoperative precaution and must not resume the destructive habit. The withdrawal will cause a nervous need for replacement, which often takes the form of excessive eating. This is a perfect time to substitute exercise, a far more positive and less dangerous habit. A structured program may require some professional guidance at the start and will become a passion as results are seen. This will curb appetite by several means, including physical fatigue, and the unwillingness to undo the good one has worked so hard to achieve. The program should include significant low-impact aerobic exercise in the form of walking, bicycling, or swimming. Muscle-building and tone maintenance are crucial for a forty-seven-year-old woman who has not been exercising regularly and well. This means weight training as well as aerobics. Osteoporosis and shrinking muscle mass are prevalent in sedentary women after menopause. It seems far more reasonable to be in good shape earlier, and face hormonal changes and their side effects as a stronger, healthier woman. There is considerable evidence that older individuals, men and women alike, even in their seventies and beyond, are able to build muscle mass and increase range of motion and bone density with regular exercise. It is never too late to get in shape—and surely never too early.

Nutrition

Although her weight has been stable for a year, Patricia is most definitely not in control of her diet. She must stop the habit of weight gain and loss immediately. Weight gain stretches the skin, and weight loss leaves that skin loose in all but the youngest people. Being a California girl of Mediterranean origin, Patricia has never been a consumer of animal fat. Fish, chicken, vegetables, and pasta are the mainstays of the healthy Mediterranean diet. Butter and cheese in limited quantities are fine. The big no-no is trans-fat, the backbone of most junk foods. Olive oil should be used whenever possible as a healthful, good-tasting, unsaturated fat. These guidelines are heart-smart; limiting fat creates by far the healthiest diet. Limiting, or eliminating added sugar in foods or for flavoring are a smart way to limit calories and help reduce circulating triglycerides. For Patricia's purposes, fat restriction is additionally important, since fat contains more than twice the calories in an equivalent amount of carbohydrate or protein. This simple dietary change will not force her to become a vegetarian, and it requires little sacrifice. The number of calories consumed should be halved. Patricia can live normally on 1500 calories a day. Since weight control has always been an issue, intermittent fasting would be an easily adhered to dietary routine. Eat nothing containing calories from dinner until lunch the following day reduces circulating carbohydrates and slakes the appetite. As discussed in the section on nutrition, there is no harm whatever in a healthy person skipping breakfast. Coffee, tea, or water can easily carry one through to lunch, and miracle of miracles, when lunchtime arrives one is not at all ravenously hungry. She should consult charts to learn her appropriate BMI range and the caloric value of the foods she enjoys. In this way, Patricia will be better able to maintain her optimal weight, and who knows—as a side benefit, she may just live longer.

Supplements

Daily: Vitamin C, 1000 milligrams; 800 IU vitamin D, optional.

Skin-Care Routine

Morning: Patricia needs to find ground zero in her routine. The copious oil production of youth has declined, though areas such as her nose and forehead tend to glisten as the day wears on. She still has little need for moisturizers and still possesses the best moisturizer of all, her own lubricating oils, which are well balanced and proper for her skin. She has no problem with allergy or irritation. (Some people actually react negatively to their own skin oils. This condition is a form of seborrhea and is one of the few conditions in which one's own oils are not the best choice.) Patricia, with her rich, natural skin oils, is the perfect candidate for a surfactant-free cleanser like *Youth Corridor Dual Action Cleanser*, or other non-foaming cleansers which will leave the protective basal lipid layer intact. After cleansing she applies *Youth Corridor Ultimate Antioxidant C* serum followed by sunscreen and the moisturizer of choice. Sunscreen is imperative in a sunny, southwestern climate. Sunscreen must be replenished regularly during outdoor activities. If there is an oil buildup on the nose or forehead, repeated washing, or cleansing is permissible. This is frequently required in warm climates with moderate humidity. The oil level of the rest of the face may need an occasional boost—but this will be the exception, not the rule.

Evening: Wash with cleanser. Apply skin-brightening serum to entire face and neck. *Youth Corridor Retinultimate* gel is perfect for this purpose. It brightens and evens skin tones, corrects fine wrinkles and prevents and treats skin eruptions. Follow with soothing moisturizer if necessary. Antioxidant serum may be applied at night if one chooses, but should be used only once daily.

Summary

Patricia is the sort of individual who will find the greatest improvement from surgical tightening of the loose skin, laser resurfacing, and fat transfer to her lip lines. She is otherwise blessed with healthy, moist, unlined skin, and requires only a good skin care routine and lifestyle reeducation to avoid making matters worse at a time in her life when they might not be so easily corrected. At this point, her appearance will be remarkably youthful for a forty-seven-year-old woman. She should not require further surgical intervention for a decade, when she will consider tightening the youth restoring lift.

Patricia would be well served by monthly visits for professional skin care. A concentrated glycolic acid peel like the *No Peel Peel* should become part of her routine, providing excellent exfoliation, and encouraging collagen growth. Microneedling with PRP will help restore a smooth, youthful upper lip.

ELLEN

Ellen is twenty-six years old and has moved to New York from Miami. She has worked as a catalogue model, and for professional and personal reasons is very aware of her appearance. She is tall, thin, fair-skinned, athletic, and very attractive. Best of all, the camera loves her high cheekbones and angular face. Ellen inherited these features from her Scandinavian mother, and shares them with much of her extended family. Unfortunately, she saw her mother age "overnight" and look like an old woman before reaching fifty. With this example, and an awareness of the dangers of Miami sunshine, Ellen is vigilant about protecting her skin. She is young and beautiful, and is interested in doing all she can to prevent the rapid aging her mother underwent.

Prescription

This young woman wants to adopt and effective routine before any significant changes are visible. She has suffered little ultraviolet damage and is aware of the rapid facial aging in her family.

Treatment

No specific treatments or surgical intervention of any sort are indicated. This situation requires education and prevention, and offers the opportunity to maintain a healthy youthful appearance for the next thirty years and beyond. The skin-care routine that follows will be Ellen's prescription for youthful skin.

Exercise

Encouraging exercise in this case is unnecessary. Ellen swims, skis, works out and plays tennis—all excellent activities. She should be counseled against doing any more than the occasional running she does on weekends and encouraged to substitute low-impact aerobic activities such as distance swimming and cycling as substitutes. Ellen's generation understands the value of exercise. She would be well-advised to make time for a daily routine, even as she assumes the rigorous schedule of early calls for work. Everyone, of every age, should be encouraged to do moderate weight training for muscle and bone strength.

Nutrition

This is a problem. Ellen remains thin for her career and has inflicted such strict dietary rules upon herself that meals are sacrificed and maintaining a full, balanced diet is a chore. Obviously, she has enough caloric intake to meet the demands of a busy professional life and fuel her athletic activities. Therefore, little more than advice on incorporating important nutrients is indicated. Since she avoids fats and empty calories and takes vitamin supplements, nothing need be addressed at present.

Supplements

In addition to the multivitamins and numerous fad additives to which Ellen periodically subscribes, she should add vitamin C, 1000 milligrams, and 800 IU vitamin D, optional.

Skin-Care Routine

Ellen has fair skin, which she has protected from the sun since childhood. She is quite expert in the use of cosmetics and removes them with industrial-strength cleansers. She has shunned the use of simple soap and water since entering her profession and has spent the majority of working days covered in various forms of stage makeup. She has a special need to find ground zero and treat her skin sensibly. That includes the removal of makeup with gentle but effective cleansers followed by vigorous towel drying. Ellen needs an emulsifier-free cleanser like *Youth Corridor Dual Action Cleanser*. Even a thorough soap-and-water wash in the morning is inadequate due to residual work-related makeup. Using cleanser twice a day again makes the case for non-foaming, emulsifier-free cleansers, which will clean effectively, but not disrupt the basal lipid layer.

Morning: After cleansing apply *Youth Corridor Ultimate Antioxidant C Boost* serum, followed by a moisturizer containing SPF 30, or sunscreen then moisturizer. This is an important step to remember in virtually all climates. The incidental sun exposure has a cumulative effect and should be protected against. After moisturizer, makeup can be applied. Ellen understands good skin care and protection but must take care to fully clear her skin of makeup and denatured oils without destroying the protective basal lipid layer, then remoisturize.

Evening: Youth Corridor Dual Action Cleanser followed by a gentle wash to remove makeup and cellular and environmental debris. The weekly use of an exfoliating mask like *Youth Corridor Beta Hydroxy Mask* is strongly encouraged. Apply gentle moisture cream of choice.

Summary

Ellen needs no treatment. An intelligent preventive routine will help keep her beautiful into middle age. Though sun damage may be minimal and not readily visible, it very likely exists and can be at least partially reversed by use of antioxidant serums containing vitamins C and E. A woman like Ellen, with minimal sun damage from childhood, can enter the program early and remain gracefully ageless. As important as this is to everyone, people in Ellen's profession are aware of the need for professional skin care. Ellen should visit her skin care clinic monthly. Her needs will include an exfoliating peel like the *Youth Corridor No Peel Peel.* This is also a good place to make the case for the use of small amounts of Botox to prevent smile lines and frown lines from developing. Wrinkles are forever, so prevention makes sense.

BOB

Bob is a sixty-year-old entrepreneur. He recently married for the second time, and has two adult children and a teen-aged step-daughter. He is healthy, takes only cholesterol lowering medications and occasional Xanax tablets for sleep. Bob's weight has remained steady at 170 lbs, which on his 5'11" frame gives him a BMI of 23.7. Perfectly normal. He doesn't work out regularly, but plays tennis on weekends, runs and plays golf in the summer. He has fair skin and thinning, light hair. His issues include deep wrinkles of his cheeks and nasolabial folds and laxity of his jawline and neck. Recently he has had two basal cell carcinomas removed from his cheek and nose.

Prescription

Bob has a genetic tendency to loss of elasticity and wrinkling. This has been accelerated by sun damage long before he began regular use of sunscreen. He has no skin care routine, and has never had cosmetic surgery or professional skin care.

Treatment

The nature of Bob's skin, and the punishment inflicted by sun have precluded any not surgical option. He would benefit from a C-lift to tighten his cheek skin and jowls, and excision of submental skin to remove excess from his upper neck. Fat transfers will fill in some of the deep creases, but he will still look masculine.

Either before, or six weeks after surgery, Bob will undergo IPL treatments to rid his skin of hyperpigmentation and age spots.

Exercise

Bob continues to enjoy sports, but at sixty running is problematic. He doesn't run enough to worry about skin elasticity, but ankles, knees, hips, and back suffer from the repeated pounding and age. It is important to substitute low impact aerobics into his routine. Bob should begin a weight routine three times weekly to maintain muscle mass and bone density.

Nutrition

Since Bob is already taking statins for cholesterol his diet should intentionally include polyunsaturated oils, like olive oil. His intake of cold water fish and vegetables should be increased, and intake of red meat limited. Perhaps most importantly, he should avoid excess refined sugar and desserts. But in general, no major alterations are prescribed.

Supplements

800IU of vitamin D is suggested at this age. 1000 mg of vitamin C, optional.

Skin Care Routine

It will be difficult to teach this old dog new tricks. Bob would benefit greatly from dermaplaning and a series of *No Peel Peels*. His fragile, fair skin requires daily use of *Youth Corridor Ultimate Antioxidant C Boost* serum. He should apply this every morning after shaving, followed by moisturizer. The combination of shaving, an excellent exfoliation, and the vitamin C serum will improve his collagen layer and help reverse sun damage.

Summary

Bob is a healthy sixty-year old fair skinned individual, who has neglected his skin. He demonstrates loss of elasticity and sun damage, which require surgery, IPL therapy, and a modest skin care routine to reverse the damage and help maintain what he has achieved. As with most men, Bob derives the benefit daily shaving which exfoliates dead cells and debris on his cheeks and neck.

THIRTEEN

Personal Checklist

The course of facial aging is generally quite predictable. Individual variations do occur. They are usually related to one's genetic makeup and, ever more frequently, lifestyle. We must understand that the inexorable course of events will affect all of us in our own special way. But it will leave none of us untouched. If some aspect of facial aging appears earlier in your mirror than your neighbor's, then find solace in the fact that the pace and the place may vary, but no one is immune. Rather than take issue with the menu of changes, understand them to be the general arc of things. In many specifics, you will find yourself ahead of or behind the curve. Whatever the case, you will find much of yourself in the following. And if you find it disturbing in its accuracy, be consoled by the knowledge that there is something you can do about every aspect of what we will be discussing.

Here is how this section works. The individual checklist is fairly difficult to face. It offers nothing reassuring other than unchecked spaces representing problems you don't yet have; otherwise, it is your own reality we are out to discover. It will help establish your position and identify problems that must be accepted or dealt with. All the symptoms can be dealt with, and the solutions are not necessarily onerous or frightening. The earlier one considers dealing with these issues, the less there will be to deal with. Even at later stages of life, one need not feel compelled to rush off for cosmetic surgery. That is not the primary purpose of this program, but it's a big part of this section. Resetting the clock may not be the goal for everyone. But all can benefit from the simple, age-related programs described herein. It takes little effort to avoid making things worse, and not much more to help make things better. Find your situation on the checklist; then read through the age-specific guide. This is organized at five-year intervals and represents average status—a generalization based on the broader population. Use that as your guide. If you don't fit into your age group, congratulations—you must be doing something right, or at least have picked your parents well. Read a notch younger and count your blessings. Some will find themselves on the far side of the curve. It isn't the end of the world; again, you are not a prisoner of these changes. There is something you can do about each and every one of them, but first, you must see the pattern clearly and determine its importance in your life.

I do not believe a desperate attempt to correct each sign of facial aging is appropriate. Surely, the reality of all this is difficult enough to take without enduring the philosophy of some weird plastic surgeon. But having lived in this odd little circumscribed environment for four decades, certain truths have become apparent to me. If you feel vital at any age, a goal of this exercise should be to look at least as good on the outside as you feel on the inside. And indeed, looking good will make you feel better as well. We want to help you to age slowly, gracefully, and beautifully, and to avoid accelerating the process with destructive behavior. I applaud any attempt to skew the curve and retard aging, but remember: The result must look natural, or it isn't worth doing. Relentless pursuit of youth, unmodified by common sense, becomes a caricature and by its own nature is self-defeating. There is little excuse for such behavior. Nor does there appear to be common sense in aggravating the aging process by refusing to unlearn bad habits or declining to make small efforts to reap rich dividends in a healthy and attractive appearance.

The following information is organized to include self-help, noninvasive treatments and cosmetic surgery. Even if you elect not to consider the treatment or surgical options, you will still benefit greatly from adopting the Youth Corridor skin-care routine. Read on, consider the information, and pursue what you wish to pursue. Each time you put off helping yourself is a day of looking better you have wasted.

THE CHECKLIST

Here is how this section works. Look closely at yourself. Be critical. Check off what you see. None of the good things about you are listed, so don't look for them; the point here is to address the unpleasant changes that time has brought.

- **Smile lines at corners of eyes**
- **Fine wrinkles beneath eyes**
- **Discolored patches on skin**
- **Dry areas or fine wrinkles on cheeks**
- **Irregularities on skin surface**
- **Sunspots on skin**
- **Irregular pigmentation on face**
- **Dark circles under eyes**

The above are simple problems that can be easily improved or corrected with a proper skin-care routine, although in some cases the process may need to be jump-started through a series of treatments by an aesthetician. Antioxidants, AHA peels, and tretinoin can reverse much of the above. Regular use of antioxidant serum can reverse much of the visible and hidden sun damage. But these are minimal skin changes, and you can make them disappear.

Correcting the findings in the next portion of the checklist require minimal intervention and fall into the category of maintenance.

- **Deeper smile lines**
- **Early vertical frown lines between the eyebrows**
- **Visible horizontal lines on the forehead**
- **Nasolabial folds**
- **Early "parentheses" at the corners of the mouth**
- **Wrinkled lower eyelids**
- **Early vertical lines on the upper lip**

Botox, fillers, and peels can control all of the above. It is important to use these minimally invasive treatments now…before the lines are etched into the skin. Continue the Youth Corridor routine for maintenance.

The third group of changes is a bit more advanced and requires various levels of intervention.

- **Excess skin of upper eyelids; hooding of eyelids**
- **Bags or puffiness under eyes**
- **Deep groove or trough under eyes**
- **Deep nasolabial fold with etched line in skin**
- **Groove from corners of mouth toward chin**
- **Double chin**
- **Jawline no longer "clean"; slight jowls**
- **Deep vertical frown lines between eyebrows**
- **Loss of cheekbone prominence**
- **Sagging cheek skin**
- **Platysma (vertical) bands at front of neck**

Each of the above represents a loss of skin tone and elasticity and requires surgical correction. The good news is that all are easily corrected, and you may be able to erase a decade, or more, of aging and start fresh. At this stage, as at any stage, adherence to the Youth Corridor skin-care routine is imperative.

Observe the descriptions that pertain to you and check them off. For the most part, you will find that your symptoms cluster in one of the three groups. The methods for dealing with the various problems have all been discussed in the chapters on the skin-care routine, over-the-counter preparations, minimally invasive treatments and surgery.

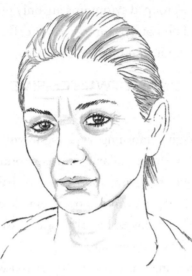

Later stages of changes are more advanced.

If the changes you see are limited to the first group, they can all be dealt with by adopting a good skin-care routine. At most, they might require a visit to an aesthetician to move things along more quickly.

If you find yourself in the second group, you need all of the above (skin-care regimen and aesthetician) and you will need minimally invasive treatments by a dermatologist or plastic surgeon. You can still hold off surgery, but you need to reverse the changes immediately, and establish this as part of your routine.

Changes in the third group can be dealt with only by a plastic surgeon. It's not a big deal; the procedures are quite routine, and you'll do just fine. Look for an experienced surgeon with a good reputation who is on your wavelength. It makes no sense to put yourself in the hands of a surgeon who doesn't understand your goals.

Having set the stage, we will next go through the personal programs for every age group. Remember, the groupings are artificial and just a general guideline. The personal programs begin with ages under twenty-five and continue to sixty and beyond. The routines should be begun as early as possible in adult life. Start before any changes are visible to keep them at bay longer than you ever imagined. From age twenty-five forward, the program will change in five-year increments. Remember: The age-grouped symptoms are only generalizations. They are not absolute and do not pertain to everyone. Find the changes that best reflect your situation and proceed from there.

UNDER TWENTY-FIVE

Skin-Care Routine:

Cleanse thoroughly morning and night with a surfactant-free cleanser, which will remove makeup and environmental free radicals from the skin, while preserving the protective basal lipid layer. You may use mild soap in the morning shower, but cleanser is necessary at night. Use warm water, followed by cold rinse. Towel-dry in an upward or lateral direction. Never downward.

Make a habit of using sunscreen whenever you will be spending any time outdoors. Not just on weekends. A moisturizer containing sunscreen eliminates a step, and keeps you from forgetting sun protection. For outdoor activities, sunscreen SPF 30 in a moisturizer base is adequate. Apply liberally half an hour before exposure. Replenish as necessary. Use water-resistant or waterproof sunscreen for swimming. Suntan creams, oils, and self-tanners are not sunscreens; most offer no protection at all.

You should apply antioxidants to your skin daily. Antioxidant combinations like vitamin C, vitamin E, and Melatonin in *Youth Corridor Ultimate C Antioxidant Boost* help with sun protection by neutralizing free radicals. Antioxidants reverse collagen breakdown, encourage new collagen production and keep your skin young.

Find a pleasing moisture cream for regular use and get in the habit. Preparations with AHA help exfoliate the dead cell layer of the skin and should be started as well. At this age, antioxidant serum, sunscreen, and AHA exfoliants are your most important tools. Professional exfoliating peels should be performed on a regular basis.

Between the teenage years and mid-twenties, skin changes abound. Oil-rich skin becomes less so, and for most the awful acne breakouts are a thing of the past. Benzyl peroxide and beta hydroxy acids were for many years the only worthwhile acne treatments. *Youth Corridor Retinultimate* is a superb anti-acne gel, perhaps the most effective over the counter preparation, but it is far more expensive than beta hydroxy preparations, or benzyl peroxide. Try the cheap ones first. In one's early twenties acne treatment may occasionally be necessary. Nasal and forehead skin may still be oily even when remoisturizing the cheeks has already become necessary. Your skin is still in turmoil; birth control pills can cause the brown mask of melasma. You haven't fully outgrown teenage problems, yet mature ones are already on the horizon. It isn't fair, but everyone goes through it. These, and other emerging skin problems, should be discussed with your dermatologist.

Exercise:

This is the time to develop a vigorous, low-impact exercise routine. Weight training and aerobic exercise are essential for physical and, I believe, mental health. Find a sport that you love and make it part of your life. You can play tennis and golf forever, and the more you learn now, the better and more sought-after you will be. Vigorous sports like skiing and cycling are great and demand that you be in good physical shape, and that's a side benefit. Through all this, protect your skin.

Diet:

You are not a kid anymore; stop eating like one. Binge-eating and crash diets are for kids. Establish sensible eating habits now. No more trans fats. Cut down on animal fats and other saturated fats. Olive oil is your friend. It tastes great and promotes cardiovascular health. You can be a vegetarian and still eat all the protein, fat, and carbohydrates your body needs. Read through the nutrition section and get a handle on how to find a healthy food regimen. Don't beat yourself up for going off your diet once in a while; we are all human, and that's life. Don't fool yourself about your caloric needs simply because you are young and active. Fifteen minutes on the rowing machine consumes barely fifty calories. How depressing.

TWENTY-FIVE

Conditions:

Skin characteristics will be virtually unchanged from above except for a decreasing susceptibility to acne like eruptions. These require a dermatologist's care. Skin may become slightly drier. No visible changes in the form of wrinkles or lines, but irregularities of the surface and slight discolorations may be present. In the dermis, collagen, and elastin, which provide the resilience of the skin, are already damaged, though no outward signs can yet be seen. The majority of the sun damage to one's skin has already been done, though an ultraviolet lamp is necessary to see it. Collagen has broken down and impending blemishes are gathering strength.

Twenty-five:
No visible changes, though biochemical denaturing of
collagen has begun.

Skin-Care Routine:

Morning: Use a surfactant-free cleanser. Those are the ones that don't foam, don't pollute the water, and don't destroy the important basal lipid layer. Mild soap once a day is not a tragedy, particularly for young people with abundant skin oils. Wash with warm water followed by cool rinse. Towel dry in an upward or lateral direction. Never downward. Apply *Youth Corridor Ultimate Antioxidant C Boost* serum. Apply moisturizer with SPF 30, or sunscreen and moisturizer separately.

Reapply moisturizer as necessary during the day. If you are spending significant time outdoors you may need to reapply sunscreen.

Evening: Wash with gentle, non-foaming cleanser to remove makeup, and cellular and environmental debris. If antioxidant serum was not applied in the morning it should be applied now to clean, dry skin. Then apply skin brightener and soothing moisturizer. This is particularly important during winter months in northern climates when low humidity and heating are particularly drying.

Nutrition:

This is the time in life to begin weight stabilization. Growth and teenage hormones are under control, and there should be little variation in weight going forward to middle age. The value of a low-fat diet and increased fruit and vegetable intake must become a habit from this point. There is nothing wrong with eating a steak, but that should become the exception not the rule. Apples are a far better snack than potato chips.

Antioxidants in food such as lycopene in tomatoes and other fruits and vegetables should be intentionally included in your diet. Omega-3 fatty acids are essential fats that cannot be manufactured by the body and must be provided by diet. They are found in cold water fish like salmon, herring, and mackerel and are important for heart health. Read about sensible dietary habits, find a pleasant routine, and stick to it. Learn to understand your caloric requirements. You need far fewer calories than you think.

Supplements:

Vitamin C, 1000 milligrams daily. Vitamin D 800 units, optional.

Exercise:

Exercise should be vigorous, both at sport and for conditioning. Aerobic activity can be unrestricted, but adopt a low-impact program. A regular, every-other-day workout routine should include aerobic activity and weight training.

THIRTY

Conditions:

The first signs of smile lines appear at the corners of the eyes. Lower lids may show a few lines below the lashes. An upper-eyelid fold of skin is visible when eyes open, with little or no overhang. Skin condition is slightly drier. As at age twenty-five, there are significant changes taking place within the collagen and elastin of the dermis. These are first demonstrated at this point as fine lines around the eyes and perhaps the beginning of a nasolabial fold, indicating early loss of elasticity. These changes are rarely significant.

Skin-Care Routine:

Morning: Wash with mild soap or gentle cleanser. Towel-dry in an upward direction for exfoliation of dead cells. Apply *Youth Corridor Ultimate Antioxidant C Boost*, or other effective vitamin C serum to face, neck, and hands. Apply moisturizer containing SPF 30 before makeup.

Evening: Wash off makeup and cellular and environmental debris with gentle cleanser like. Apply antioxidant serum to face, neck, and hands, unless this has already been applied in the morning. Use only once daily. Apply skin brightener to face, followed by gentle moisturizer. If early color irregularities or fine wrinkles are apparent begin treatment with nightly *Youth Corridor Retinultimate* gel applied to clean skin.

Nutrition:

This is a particularly important period, in which positive habits and routines must be learned. Job stress, sex, marriage, and childbirth compete for time and attention during these years. Weight changes, frequently weight gain, often occur. Weight optimization and stabilization are more easily learned now than later. An adequate and varied diet based primarily on fruits, vegetables, and complex carbohydrates is necessary for the above reasons as well as for provision of naturally occurring antioxidants and avoidance of detrimental food groups containing saturated fats and trans fats. In other words, no more junk food.

Supplements:

Vitamin C, 1000 milligrams daily; 400 IU vitamin D, optional.

Exercise:

Vigorous activities and all sports are encouraged. Avoid all high-impact activities. Swim, fast-walk, bike. Curtail distance running. Weight training for muscle tone should be part of your routine. Not only does good muscle tone contribute to healthy good looks, but it also increases and protects bone density and is a good hedge for the future.

Corrective procedures:

These are rarely necessary at this point. Toward the end of this period, as the individual approaches thirty-five, the first changes requiring the consideration of intervention arise. For most, these will be centered on the eyelid area. With the institution of good care in the form of antioxidant serums, retinoids, or tretinoin, AHA masks, or preferably a jump start on new skin with concentrated AHA peels. These efforts will push back the need for intervention.

THIRTY-FIVE

Conditions:

During this period, skin will become dryer than in the past. Smile lines about the eyes may become noticeable. Nasolabial lines will deepen a bit and approach the corners of the mouth. For many, vertical frown lines between the eyebrows will appear and deepen. Upper eyelids appear heavier. Excess skin of the upper eyelids will appear to varying degrees, and the lower-lid area will become puffier more often. There is little significant loosening of the skin, but damage to collagen will have occurred, and fullness may be developing in the lower face. This represents early loss of elasticity.

In general, these changes will be manifested to some degree during the period from thirty-five to forty. The changes, when they occur, are in the early stages and, though not terrible, are a sign of a new stage in life.

Thirty to thirty-five:
Fine lines around eyes and early nasolabial folds.

Skin-Care Routine:

Morning: Wash thoroughly with mild soap or non-foaming cleanser. Use warm water, followed by cold splash. Towel-dry in an upward direction.

Apply *Youth Corridor Ultimate Antioxidant C Boost* serum to face, neck and back of hands. Apply skin brightener to face, followed by moisturizer with SPF 30 before makeup.

Evening: Wash off makeup and cellular and environmental debris with gentle skin cleanser. Apply antioxidant skin serum to face, neck, and back of hands, unless already applied in morning. Use only once daily. Apply skin brightener, followed by gentle moisturizer. Enriched eye cream should be used around eye area to combat early wrinkles.

If necessary, begin use of retinoid like *Youth Corridor Retinultimate gel* in smile lines and under eye area to treat early wrinkles. In more severe wrinkling tretinoin (Retin-A) can be applied to under-eye and smile-line areas. (With regular use of antioxidant serum and *Retinultimate* this will not be necessary. You can probably save it for later in life.) Tretinoin works by increasing the rate of cell turnover, and in the back of my mind is the notion that there are a finite number of cell turnovers possible, so it might not be the best idea to speed them up until absolutely necessary. Antioxidants and AHA creams can help with most case fine wrinkles. AHA peels and IPL laser treatments are particularly good to restore skin clarity and reduce fine lines, and help you return to baseline.

Sunscreen must be applied whenever you use tretinoin, as skin discoloration from the sun exposure is possible, which is another reason to apply it at night.

Procedures:

Botox may be appropriate. If you smile or frown and the lines persist after the moment of expression has passed, you should begin to do something about it before the lines become etched into your skin. Otherwise, hold off. Several small procedures can do a great deal to stop the changes between thirty-five and forty. AHA peels for smile lines and under-eye wrinkles are very effective. Fat transfers are excellent for treating the deepening nasolabial folds and diminish them before they become etched into the skin. Fillers can be used for the same purpose but will have to be repeated two or three times yearly. Fat transfers can halt the problem for a decade, or more. This is the right time to treat softening of the jawline and under-chin area with microsuction for immediate relief before the problem escalates.

Nutrition:

As discussed previously, this period continues to be the most physically demanding. Professional responsibilities, pregnancy and child rearing, and a wealth of physical demands accrue. It is a particularly important period during which to maintain control. There are so many reasons and excuses for forgetting about nutrition and exercise for a while, and getting on with the important things in life, that we lose sight of the fact that these *are* among the important things in life. Good nutrition should have become a part of your life by now. A salad and fresh fruit are as easily accessible as cookies and ice cream, and not only are they far healthier, but they also set a good example. Perhaps your family won't have to unlearn dietary habits as we had to. With fewer calories being spent on physical activities, caloric intake should be carefully controlled. For most women, this becomes a period when dietary extremes take over. Neither denial nor indulgence is acceptable, though viewed from the perspective of facial aging, more damage is done by excessive weight, which stretches and breaks down elastic fibers, than by being too thin, which, if not carried to an unhealthy extreme, results only in an unattractive appearance, and can easily be corrected with weight gain. In any event, thirty-five to forty is not the time to experiment. If your tendency is to weight gain, experiment with intermittent fasting, discussed in the nutrition section. By withholding calories between dinner and lunch the body is encouraged to burn fat. The side effect is your appetite is reduced by lunchtime. Yes, it means skipping breakfast.

Once again: Reduce your calorie intake. Remember, you very likely need no more than about 1500 calories a day to sustain a normal lifestyle; low-fat, high-complex-carbohydrate diets with adequate protein are the rule. Limit the amount of protein from animal sources other than cold water fish like salmon and mackerel, which are great sources of omega-3 fatty acid. Use unsaturated fats such as olive oil in your salad dressing and for cooking. Fresh fruit and vegetables are increasingly important as a source of vitamins and nutrients not readily supplied by supplements.

Supplements:

Vitamin C, 1000 milligrams daily; 800 IU vitamin D, optional.

Exercise:

Although life's demands make it increasingly difficult to participate, physical activities are crucial. This is the time to maintain conditioning and fitness. What is lost here becomes increasingly difficult to regain.

Running, other than a short-distance warm-up, or occasional serious run, should gradually be abandoned in favor of any other aerobic workout. Bicycling, fast walking, and swimming are encouraged. Stair-climbing machines, elliptical trainers, and rowing machines, among other devices, provide good aerobic workouts but are dependent on availability and physical condition. Simply walking briskly for twenty minutes per day provides enough aerobic exercise for cardiac protection, but that is not enough activity for age thirty-five to forty year old. Active sports and weight training are essential for your future physical well-being and pretty good for your mental health as well. Two forty-five-minute workouts per week will maintain muscle tone. Three will build muscle and strength. Don't worry about becoming muscle-bound; this won't do it.

FORTY

Conditions:

The transition from thirty-five to forty is far less dramatic physically than emotionally. While one may consider this a major milestone on the road to maturity, the aging process has actually preceded it. During the years from forty to forty-five, changes hinted at several years earlier slowly amplify. Nasolabial folds deepen. Eyelid skin loosening becomes noticeable when applying eye makeup. Wrinkles around eyes deepen. There is a slight loosening of skin at the jawline and below, and perhaps, fat accumulation. Fine wrinkles and blemishes are particularly evident on fair-skinned individuals. Vertical lines between eyebrows deepen, and tiny vertical lines may be noted on the upper lip, but these things are often lost in a youthful overall appearance, which may allow them to go unheeded until they become unavoidable. This is unfortunate, because now is the time when these changes can be halted and easily reversed.

Thirty-five to forty:
Smile lines, deepening nasolabial fold, vertical frown
lines and some excess eyelid skin.

Skin-Care Routine:

Morning: Wash with mild soap or cleanser. Towel-dry with upward motion. Apply *Youth Corridor Ultimate Antioxidant C Boost* or other effective vitamin C serum. Apply skin brightener and eye cream containing AHA or peptides, and moisturizer containing SPF 30 before makeup.

Evening: Use gentle cleanser to remove makeup and environmental and cellular debris. Unless applied in the morning, apply antioxidant serum to face, neck, and backs of hands. Begin use of *Youth Corridor Retinultimate* gel to areas of fine lines and skin color irregularities. If lines are becoming unusually deep a course of tretinoin (Retin-A) may be necessary. Follow treatment with a rich moisturizer. Eye and neck cream are indicated if early wrinkling of neck skin has become noticeable.

Weekly home use of AHA peel or masks should be begun.

Procedures:

Nothing major is yet required. Begin the routine of professional AHA peels performed by an aesthetician will help skin look its best. For men and women in this age group a series of three 70-percent glycolic acid *Youth Corridor No Peel Peel* jump starts the antiaging process. Superficial laser, or IPL treatments, help return blemish-free luster to the skin. The home skin-care routine works to augment and protect the result.

Fillers become necessary for nasolabial folds and vertical frown lines. I believe the most natural and best of the fillers is autologous fat transfer, and although it is more costly initially and more time-consuming to perform, it offers long-term relief from the problem. The cheekbone area may be highlighted by fat transfers as well. Remember, in most cases an estimated 30 to 35 percent of the injected fat will be retained permanently, so even the best results will need to be repeated. Most people find two fat transfers over the course of a year offer enough permanent correction for a decade. Botox can be administered for treatment of smile lines and forehead wrinkles as necessary.

Microsuction may be indicated to reverse softening of the jawline and early jowls or double chin. If there is significant excess upper eyelid skin, it should be excised. Puffiness of lower eyelid area can be treated with subconjunctival blepharoplasty. TCA peel or laser resurfacing of the lower eyelid area may be necessary, if wrinkles or dark circles are significant. Often much of the tired look and dark circles can be eliminated by simply filling in the deep tear trough where the lower eyelid skin meets the cheek.

Nutrition:

As mentioned for younger age groups, a low-fat diet based primarily on grains, complex carbohydrates, fruits, vegetables, and fish will provide all the elements of good nutrition. Caloric intake is more easily controlled with this sort of diet and should already have become a habit. Fat restriction begun earlier now becomes doubly important, as estrogen, and for men, testosterone, levels deplete over this decade. Nutritional habits begun earlier are important for all aspects of overall health.

Supplements:

Vitamin C, 1000 milligrams daily; 800 IU vitamin D, optional.

Exercise:

Active sports become less important as a source of aerobic conditioning as time becomes increasingly scarce; it must be replaced by strict exercise programs. These should include impact-free aerobics and range-of-motion and strength training. Routines must be performed at least three times weekly to meet goals. Twenty minutes of walking, swimming, rowing or bicycling can be performed daily. Weight training should be performed three times per week.

If strength-building routines are done daily, the muscle groups exercised should alternate. Muscles need a day of rest to recover from vigorous exercise. If the exercise performed has not been vigorous and strenuous, its value will be diminished. It is important not to continually increase the weight lifted. At some point, this will build bulkier muscle mass, which may not be the goal you have in mind. Weight training is important from this point forward to help maintain bone density. Whenever possible, it is best to establish exercise routines with a qualified fitness trainer.

FORTY-FIVE

Conditions:

The last five years of the decade from forty to fifty witness the loss of the battle with gravity. The process cannot be denied, though it differs greatly between individuals. Collagen and elastin denature, stretch, and break. In most cases, this has been accelerated by lifestyle. Whatever the circumstances and extent, there is loosening of the skin. Nasolabial folds become heavy, and a line may be etched into the skin from the constant, natural motion of the area if it has gone untreated in the past. Pockets of fat may develop outside the corners of the mouth, and a line or fold from the corners of the mouth begins to head downward toward the jaw, due to loose tissue above and folds and fat alongside. Cheekbones become masked, as subcutaneous padding drops below the prominence. The skin of the neck no longer bounces back from stretching, and is no longer as tight as it has been. Vertical lines deepen on the upper lip. Smile lines deepen, as do frown lines, and eyelid skin shows more excess and overhang. Fine wrinkles, more pronounced on cheeks, become deeper.

The skin around the upper eyelids has stretched and become a bit more redundant. Puffiness and wrinkles are more frequent on the lower lids. Deep frown lines may have set between the eyebrows, and the skin is less lustrous, with areas of irregular pigmentation. These changes will have become evident years earlier and should have been dealt with at the time they appeared. I mention them again to complete an accurate survey of expected changes at this stage.

To a greater or lesser degree, all these things happen. Within the next five years, the changes will accelerate and demand attention for the majority of people. Twenty years of maintenance would have done much to prevent, hold back, and mask these changes. Unfortunately, we have only recently come upon both the tools and the organization to help lead more gracefully into this period. Changes noted in the previous five-year period, to age forty-five, will be addressed again. Years of good habits would likely have had a major positive effect on maintaining the integrity of collagen and elastin, therefore significantly retarding the appearance of laxity and wrinkles.

Forty to forty-five:
Changes accelerate.

To some extent, all these things are happening. But make no mistake: At fifty you can and should look fabulous. Just pay some attention to yourself.

Skin-Care Routine:

Morning: Perform a warm wash with cleanser, or mild soap, followed by cold splash and towel-drying in upward, or lateral direction. Apply *Youth Corridor Ultimate Antioxidant C Boost*, or other effective vitamin C serum, to face, neck, and back of hands. Apply brightening serum to face, then moisturizer very rich moisturizer with SPF 30, or add sunscreen before makeup.

Evening: Wash with gentle cleanser to remove makeup and cellular and environmental debris. Apply antioxidant skin serum to face, neck, and back of hands unless used in morning routine. Use serum only once a day.

You may apply skin brightener to face, but by age fifty a more potent product, such as a *Youth Corridor Retinultimate* gel, is indicated. You should be using the vitamin C serum and a retinoid once a day, every day. Tretinoin may be required for trouble spots like under-eye wrinkles, smile lines and color irregularities. Remember, tretinoin (Retin-A) must be applied to dry skin. Follow with rejuvenating eye cream and gentle moisturizer.

Procedures:

Regular professional skin care—including AHA peels, and superficial laser resurfacing—is necessary at this point. Pigment spots should be removed as soon as they are noticed. IPL or laser can do this with no significant down time. Professional skin care should be performed in a series of six treatments two weeks apart, at least once annually. I usually suggest a 70-percent glycolic acid peel, like the *Youth Corridor No Peel Peel* because it is simple and causes no down time, but most concentrated AHA peels will do an excellent job. This will do a great deal to keep your skin looking young.

Fillers or fat transfers are necessary, and Botox will be used two or three times a year. In the years from fifty to fifty-five, the need for surgical intervention increases. By this time, most women who have not already done so are ready to have their upper and lower eyelids done. If vertical frown lines are prominent, the corrugator muscles are cut through the upper eyelid incision. If dark circles under the eyes are a problem, they can be addressed by laser resurfacing if bleaching creams have not solved the problem. The tear trough under the eye is filled with fat, or commercial filler, and the tired look is instantly corrected. Micro-suction is done for fat pockets beside the mouth and along the jawline and the double chin.

If the nasolabial folds are becoming increasingly heavy and the cheek skin is loosening, it is time to consider a limited-incision face-lift. Also known as a short-scar face-lift, this is the modern version of the mini-lift. It tightens the cheek skin and underlying tissues, significantly reverses the nasolabial folds, lifts and tightens the cheeks, and rejuvenates the jawline and upper neck. Fifty may seem young to contemplate this surgery, but we are dealing with the signs and symptoms of aging, not simply chronological age. If the changes are happening…deal with them. The result of the surgery should always be a natural, youthful look. Having the procedure performed at this stage significantly slows the clock…and turns it back a decade. It always looks more natural than the dramatic correction need at an older age.

Nutrition:

The years from forty-five to fifty-five see many metabolic changes. Calorie needs are reduced. Subcutaneous fat seems to be undergoing redistribution and gaining on us. Typically, childbearing years end and many enter the hormonal change of menopause. For men, testosterone levels have dipped, and metabolism changes as well.

Calorie intake must be closely related to needs. Significant weight gain at this juncture would result in irreversible stretching of skin. The fact that individuals at this stage of life often find themselves unable to digest heavy meals taken in the evening is an undeniable indication that the digestive and metabolic processes have changed. Just as one's needs diminish with changes in bodily function, so does the physiological ability to tolerate the intake necessary in the building years. Light meals, less protein, more fruit and vegetables, more water, and much less fat are called for.

Supplements:

Vitamin C, 1000 milligrams daily; calcium supplement, either as calcium tablets or in multivitamins, and 800 IU of vitamin D. After menopause, more than 1000 IU of vitamin D is recommended.

Exercise:

Force yourself. This is a very important period. Exercise should be vigorous enough to provide aerobic conditioning and muscle building. Good muscle size and strength are closely related to bone density, which is essential in the prevention of osteoporosis and the full enjoyment of a healthy middle life. There should be nothing physically impossible at this point in life except, perhaps, childbearing. For many reasons, your parents may have actually been old at fifty, which is unthinkable today. The first line of defense is physical activity, and this must include conditioning. Working out isn't fun, but do it now and improve the quality of the next forty years of your life.

FIFTY-FIVE TO SIXTY

Conditions:

This is the big time. There is no disguising it; things have changed—just look at what is happening to the friends around you. No more fooling around. The years from fifty to fifty-five affect the appearance of most women quite dramatically. From fifty-five to sixty it becomes a daily reminder. For most men the period is not as critical. A number of factors, such as thicker skin, beard, and shaving account for the differences, but most men, at this point, are concerned only if their skin no longer "fits."

If one kept up with the little things there would be no shocking signs of aging to contend with at fifty-five, or sixty. So far the changes have not been precipitous, just the gradual effects of aging and the onset and acceptance of menopause. You are still young and vital, so get on with the business of living.

Nothing happens at fifty-five that hasn't been creeping up on you for years. The changes are gradual. Loss of elasticity continues, and the changes described in the previous sections increase. This is simply more of the same, and it can be dealt with similarly, if a bit more aggressively.

If no surgery has been done to this point, the changes will not be dissimilar from the previous section. There will likely be excess skin and, perhaps, hooding of the upper eyelids. The lower lids will be wrinkled and perhaps puffy. Tear trough deformity deepens. Deepen is a big term going forward. Vertical frown lines between the eyebrows deepen, and become constant, and the eyebrows themselves will have dropped somewhat. Horizontal lines of the forehead are noticeably deeper. Nasolabial folds deepen, and the lines within the fold become etched into the skin. Lines deepen at corners of the mouth, accentuated by small fat pockets. Cheekbones look less prominent as subcutaneous fat padding drops. Early jowls interrupt the clean line of the jaw, and loose skin becomes evident under the chin. The platysma muscle loosens and forms two vertical bands that appear at the front of the neck. Fine wrinkled skin of the neck accumulates. Vertical lines deepen on upper lip, and wrinkles are noted on cheeks.

Fifty to fifty-five:
Changes continue. Loss of elasticity becomes noticeable.

Procedures:

Microsuction, commercial fillers or fat transfers, and Botox are already being used. Most people are fully ready to have their eyes done, if they have not already done so. The early jowls and fat deposits along the sides of the mouth may have been addressed, but laxity of the cheeks, deep nasolabial folds, and laxity of the neck are more pronounced, as is the marionette line from the outside of the mouth to the jaw. The limited-incision, or short scar, face-lift has been designed to deal with these issues and should largely erase them. It is not a miracle, but, given this stage of aging, the operation can turn back the clock more than ten years, to a time before these changes were manifested on your face. Ancillary procedures like corrugator resection are performed, if necessary.

After fifty-five, the loss of elasticity is often obvious in odd places. Earlobes stretch with gravity, often helped along by the weight of earrings, and the tip of the nose begins to point downward. Both of these issues can be simply addressed at the time of surgery, and both have an unimaginably positive impact on restoring one's youthful good looks.

Fat transfers are almost always done at the same time to fill in the wrinkles caused by the repeated action of the muscles of facial expression, such as the etched nasolabial line, upper lip lines and vertical frown lines. The lift replaces fat and local tissue on the cheekbones, but often extra fat is added to the cheekbones and chin as well to add youthful angularity.

For some in this age group, microsuction and larger volume fat transfers are all that is necessary, but that is usually the exception, not the rule. This is where genes and long-term care play a role. Good genes and good skin care mean less surgery.

Nutrition:

Nutritional standards are unchanged from forty-five. Caloric needs have diminished, and weight gain seems to result from the slightest indiscretion. Significant weight gain must be avoided, as the skin has lost elasticity and will be permanently stretched. Heavy meals are poorly digested, resulting in a feeling of lassitude, and should be avoided. By now you should have realized that the pleasant social interlude that mealtimes have become can be enjoyed without over indulgence. Fruits, vegetables, grains, and complex carbohydrates should comprise the framework of your diet. It should contain much less fat. Reduction in dietary fat reduces calories, as fat contains more than twice the calories of either protein or carbohydrates. At least as important is the fact that after menopause the incidence of heart disease in women skyrockets. This runs a parallel course with the loss of the protective effect of estrogen, and even when we believed in protection by hormone replacement, a more alert lifestyle was indicated.

Drink at least a quart of fluid daily. This does not have to be water, and there is honestly no need to carry a water bottle around all day. All liquids are water based, and your body ultimately deals with them all as water. But the additives do count, and not usually in a positive way.

Consume alcoholic beverages only within reason. There have been no large-scale studies that I know of to determine whether alcohol reduces the incidence of heart disease in postmenopausal women as it does in men, so enjoy it—but use it frugally. Although most women seem to favor white wine, red wine should be the alcoholic beverage of choice since it contains resveratrol, the seemingly magical compound that extends cell life. Unfortunately, if this is true, as it seems to be, we have no idea how much is necessary for this positive effect, so moderation is the rule.

Salad, olive oil, cooked tomatoes, green vegetables, and cold water fish are all appropriate for every reason. After age fifty, vitamin D is less efficiently absorbed from the intestines. Therefore, dietary supplements in the form of capsules or as additives to food are increasingly important, particularly as calcium metabolism and bone density become an issue during these years. A glass of milk provides 25 percent of the daily vitamin D requirement, but drinking four glasses of milk daily is a double-edged sword, considering fat and calorie content. Some non-dietary supplements become important.

Supplements:

Vitamin C, 1000 milligrams daily; calcium supplement daily; at least 1000 IU of vitamin D.

Exercise:

As active sports activities are reduced, aerobic and muscle training must increase. Aerobic fitness is cardiovascular fitness and is directly related to all forms of physical performance, from golf to sex. It is directly related to longevity and must be maintained.

If one has not worked with a trainer before, this is a great time to begin. Muscle mass and muscle tone are related to maintaining bone density and preventing osteoporosis. Exercising must become a habit. Real exercise yields real results. Don't fool yourself: Waving your arms around twice a week is not enough. Work out for 45 minutes at least three times a week. Fast-walking, walking on the inclined treadmill, bicycling, stair-climbing machines, elliptical trainers, and swimming are excellent aerobic exercises and great warm-ups for weight training. No running. If you ran before, cut down or stop. If you are not a runner, definitely do not start now.

Not only will serious workouts be crucial for your well-being, but you will look better and feel great.

Skin-Care Routine:

Skin care becomes a coordinated effort leaning heavily on professional routines. Regular series of superficial peels and laser, or ILP treatments control superficial wrinkling and unsightly pigmentation. At this stage special attention should be paid to the neck and décolletage, as well as the back of the hands. These areas of thin skin suffer greatly from sun exposure and natural attrition, and can be effectively rejuvenated by the same modalities applied to the face. Treatment series may be repeated twice yearly and provide an excellent foundation for the daily routine. Having had cosmetic surgery does not mean you can ignore skin care; you need to protect your investment in yourself.

Morning: Wash with mild soap or gentle cleanser. Towel-dry in an upward direction. Apply *Youth Corridor Ultimate C Antioxidant Boost* or other effective vitamin C serum to face, neck, décolletage, and back of hands. Apply skin brightener, followed by SPF 30 moisturizer and rejuvenating eye cream before makeup.

Evening: Wash away makeup and cellular and environmental debris with gentle cleanser. If vitamin C serum has not been applied in the morning, apply serum to face, neck, and backs of hands. Use only once daily.

Youth Corridor Retinultimate gel should be applied to face, neck, décolletage, and the back of hands. This will brighten and lighten skin, treat fine wrinkles, and equalize pigment. Tretinoin may be necessary in problem areas. Do not use tretinoin and *Retinultimate* on the same area. Apply eye cream and rich moisturizer.

AHA and BHA masks, or home peels may be used weekly.

It may be necessary to apply moisturizer more than twice daily. This should never be done over makeup. Treatment products must be applied directly to skin in order to work. Using them over makeup or moisturizer is a waste of time. It is OK to wash off makeup and remoisturize during the day. The morning treatments have already penetrated. Re-moisturize and make up, if necessary.

SIXTY, SIXTY-FIVE, AND BEYOND

Reiterating the changes in the years is boring and counterproductive. Suffice it to say that there is more of the same. Yes, it gets worse, but you can intervene and roll back the clock at any stage. Unfortunately, waiting until sixty-five to get serious is not nearly as effective as adopting a program of Prevention, Maintenance and Correction at an earlier stage. Not only will you have wasted precious decades waiting to look bad enough to do anything about the changes, but some of the signs of aging that could easily have been prevented are difficult to eradicate. Having said that, it is never too late to start.

The primary changes of the years beyond sixty are in the quality of the skin, and loss of facial padding. Never underestimate the importance of facial volume. And, like it or not, we lose volume in our faces with age. Generally, correcting the problem is easy once the problem is recognized. Fat transfers to the cheekbones, chin, and nasolabial folds do wonders, filling loose skin, heightening the infrastructure, and adding youthful angularity. Thinning, wrinkled skin is more problematic. Wrinkled cheeks and "chicken skin" on the neck are increasingly evident. As mentioned previously, these conditions respond well to antioxidants, IPL and laser resurfacing.

Cosmetic surgery is usually indicated as well. In the case of wrinkled, loose neck skin, a traditional face-lift and neck lift is required. This is more surgery than one would have needed to contemplate a few years earlier. It has been a standard procedure for generations, and today's plastic surgeons take pains to avoid the overdone, windblown face-lift look of the past.

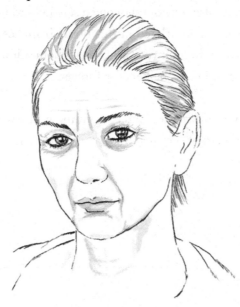

Sixty and beyond:
Loss of elasticity and wrinkling become more profound.

One might say that women waiting until they really hate the way they look before having a face-lift are getting away with just one procedure, while those who chose to have smaller procedures done along the way, will, in total, have undergone as much or more surgery.

Gerald Imber, M.D.

True enough, but they also have had twenty-five years of looking great instead of wasting twenty-five years waiting to look old enough to have a surgical face-lift at sixty-five.

Summary

Can the Youth Corridor skin-care routine and its self-help program, along with small procedures performed earlier, actually keep you looking exactly the same from thirty-five to sixty-five? Well, not exactly the same, but pretty darn close. It is not a perfect system, but to paraphrase Winston Churchill's comment about democracy: It may not be perfect, but it's better than all the others.

The Youth Corridor strategy CAN keep you looking beautiful and youthful throughout your adult years; it's as simple as that. Even if you aren't convinced of the wisdom of doing small procedures earlier, there is absolutely no excuse for not following a self-help routine, such as the program that has been outlined in this book. It makes sense, and it is the least you can do to look your best throughout adult life.

Start young and reap the benefits forever.

For more information and continuing updates, please visit:
www.Drimber.com and www.Youthcorridorclinic.com

Notes & Questions

If you have questions feel free to contact us at: www.Youthcorridorclinic.com

Notes & Questions

Notes & Questions

Notes & Questions

If you have questions feel free to contact us at: www.Youthcorridorclinic.com

Notes & Questions

If you have questions feel free to contact us at: www.Youthcorridorclinic.com

Acknowledgements

A single person can rarely take credit for scientific advances. And as much as one would like to claim credit for modest ideas that interpret what science has taught us, it is rare indeed for that to be the case. So it is with the information in, and even the concept of, this book. It is true, however, that whatever errors and misrepresentations are contained herein, are wholly, and solely my responsibility. I have endeavored to be informative, straight forward, and honest throughout. If I have missed that target, I apologize, and beg your forgiveness.

The first edition of this book was edited by Claire Wachtel, of William Morrow and Company, a division of HarperCollins. Subsequent editions and updates have built on that framework. The recent past edition was produced in standard, and video augmented formats, originally organized by Cheryl Gould at NBC Universal, and ultimately taken over and published by Michael Fabiano, who is again the publisher of the current edition. I thank them again, and all the people who have helped along the way. Bill Jobson produced illustrations and designs.

About the
Author

D r. Gerald Imber is rated among the top one percent of plastic surgeons by Castle Connolly and U.S. News, and is an acknowledged authority on antiaging and beauty. Since the initial publication of The Youth Corridor, nearly twenty years ago, his strategy of Prevention, maintenance, and Correction has helped many thousands of followers maintain their youthful good looks throughout adult life.

Dr. Imber is the author of numerous books and scientific papers. His numerous contributions include the Limited Incision facelift Technique, and implementing and popularizing microsuction.

In addition to his surgical practice, Dr. Imber is the director of the Youth Corridor Clinic.

For more information see www.Drimber.com, and www.Youthcorridorclinic.com.

CPSIA information can be obtained
at www.ICGtesting.com
Printed in the USA
LVOW04s1154260317
528501LV00004B/94/P